CW00858100

SILLY ISLAND

By

Brian Beresford

ISBN: 978-1-914933-66-0

www.i2ipublishing.co.uk

i2i Publishing, Manchester.

Contents

Chapters:

Six-year-old Spring looked around her classroom. Each child had been given a piece of paper no bigger than a page from this book on which to use crayons to draw a duck wearing a lifejacket. Spring saw that the others all looked so happy, giggling away as they did exactly what the teacher had told them to do. But she didn't feel like doing that, and when her teacher came near, she told her how she felt. "Please can I have a giant piece of paper, every colour of paint and big thick brushes? I want to paint a life-size picture of my whole family, please."

"I'm sorry, Spring," the teacher said. "In today's silly art lesson we are all using crayons to draw ducks wearing lifejackets because it's a silly thing to do. When you are ten, you will be in Mr Acrylic's class, and he will show you how to paint on bigger paper."

Spring didn't want to wait four years. She desperately wanted to paint an enormous picture of her family right now, but she kept her thoughts to herself, picked up the crayons and quickly drew a duck wearing a lifejacket. Then she folded her arms, closed her eyes and imagined being in her own bedroom, painting a life-size picture of her family on the ceiling.

"Just you wait!" she said to herself. "Just you wait!"

1.The Podcast

Gerald Grainger: Welcome to the latest in our series of UK21 Radio podcasts, in which I interview world leaders from my studio in the United Kingdom. Today I'm chatting to a lady who is the elected leader of a small island many of you may not have heard of. Her name is Lollipop McNoodly-Noodly and she has recently been chosen to lead Silly Island for the next five years. Good morning, Lollipop.

Lollipop McNoodly-Noodly: Good morning to you too, Gerald. This is the first time I have ever been interviewed by someone who isn't from Silly Island, and I must apologise if I sometimes turn into a prickly cactus while you are speaking.

Gerald: What on earth do you mean?

Lollipop: Yes, we are on Earth, but if I spend too long worrying about turning into a prickly cactus, we won't get anything done, will we? So where are you hiding now?

Gerald: I assure you, I'm not hiding, and I'm speaking to you from far away by using the wonders of satellite technology to transmit my voice to you on

Silly Island. Speaking of which, where precisely is Silly Island?

Lollipop: Silly Island is somewhere near the middle of the greatest ocean, and I am sitting on a pumpkin somewhere near the middle of my kitchen, which is somewhere near the middle of my house, which is somewhere near the middle of Sillytown, which is somewhere near the middle of Silly Island.

Gerald: Let me ask you a two-part question. How big is Silly Island, and for how long have you lived there?

Lollipop: Let me give you a three-part answer. Firstly, Silly Island is far bigger than an ant, but far smaller than the entire universe. It is approximatelymatelymately the size of the Isle of Skye. Secondully, I have lived on Silly Island all my life, other than when I jump into the air, at which point I suppose I'm not actually on Silly Island but somewhere above it. You must guess my age, but I'll tell you that the answer is either four seconds, thirty-four years or six hundred and forty-two thousand years; and thirdly, I think I am about to turn into a prickly cactus, for which I hereby apologise.

Gerald: Is it true that everyone on Silly Island is silly?

Lollipop: Of course, Raymond.

Gerald: My name isn't Raymond, it's Gerald, Lollipop.

Lollipop: Your name is Gerald Lollipop? Wow, that's such a coincidence because I'm called Lollipop, Gerald. We both have the same names, but in different orders!

Gerald: I thought your name was Lollipop McNoodly-Noodly.

Lollipop: Oh yes, of course. Thank you for reminding me. I get awfully confused about steam-powered vacuum cleaners, you know.

Gerald: So, why does everyone have to be silly on Silly Island?

Lollipop: That's a silly question, but not as silly as this one - can flannels survive at temperatures below freezing point? An even sillier question would be, who was the first person to sail round the world on a packet of nasturtium seeds? Your question is not really very silly at all, but I shall answer it for you before I turn into a prickly cactus. Everyone on Silly

Island can be silly at any time they like, but on Hippetyscringeday (which I believe you call Thursday) they must try their hardest to be silly all the time.

Gerald: Very interesting.

Lollipop: No, it isn't.

Gerald: It is to me, and I'm sure our listeners would like to know why all the islanders must be silly for a lot of their lives.

Lollipop: Isn't it obvious, Ethel? (I hope you don't mind me calling you Ethel - let's be honest, it's much better than being called Footnosetomato.) When people are being silly they smile more, they laugh more, they care more and they are happier. They don't get angry, they never argue or fight, tell lies, bully each other or commit crimes. It's wonderful to live on Silly Island! You should come to live here, Ethel, and see for yourself.

Gerald: Do children on Silly Island have to go to school?

Lollipop: They do! Being silly is a serious subject and it is taught for half of the time the children are in school. But, of course, no-one goes to school on Hippetyscringedays, because that's the day when everyone can be silly all the time, and it gives the children a chance to show how much silliness they have learnt in school. By the way, I'm not turning into a prickly cactus at the moment, but I think one of my prickly cacti is trying to turn into me. Botheration!

Gerald: I must say, I think that we all need happiness in our lives, and if Silly Island leads the way in how to find it, we could all learn a lot from you.

Lollipop: "Krang krang krang krang," remarked the noisy cabbage.

Gerald: Are there any rules about how to be silly, or can people just do what they like?

Lollipop: Your moustache is starting to crawl up your face. Oh, sorry, I should answer your question. People must never be silly in a way that could hurt another person or their property, they must never be nasty to each other or to animals, they must not tell lies and they must never make a mess without cleaning it up.

Gerald: Silly Island sounds wonderful to me, Lollipop, but is there a downside to living there?

Lollipop: Two of the best things about Silly Island are also two of the worst things. Number one, there is hardly ever any breeze on Silly Island, and we have no idea what a wind feels like. Number two, there are hardly ever any waves on the sea around the island. Number three, there isn't a number three.

Gerald: How can it be a bad thing to not have wind or waves?

Lollipop: We have seen pictures of people in other countries flying kites, blowing bubbles and riding surfboards. We would love to try those happy things and could do them all in very silly ways indeed, but it's not possible to do them here.

Gerald: Do the adults on Silly Island have to go to work?

Lollipop: Your moustache has run away now! Send your cat out to bring it home before it reaches the forests: lots of lost moustaches set up their own communities in the forests. Yes, everyone goes to work here, apart from on Hippetyscringedays, when they are all silly all the time. Most people work in the coal mine at Dimble, but there is probably only five years' supply of coal left, and in any case, we have discovered that mining coal and other fossil fuels is a bad thing to do, and we should be using alternative energy to produce electricity. We just can't use electricity when we want to these days, and on Hippetyscringedays we try to use it as little as possible; we have to be silly in ways that don't need electricity.

Gerald: That must be a huge problem for you. Have you tried to use alternative sources of energy to generate electricity?

Lollipop: Pots and pans may break my shovel, but trowels will never desert me. A very very very very very very very very very very very very very very very very very very very very very very very very very very very very very very very very very very very very very very very very very very very very very very very very very very very very very very very very very very very very very very very very very rich man called Basil Herb (his name was Basil Blake before he came here) arrived at Silly Island three years ago. He told us he would solve our problem. He spent two years building something in an underground factory and then invited everyone (except the Yllis family, who were having a false nose evening in their shed) to the grand unveiling of his invention. All ten thousand, four hundred and eight of us went to Friendly Shirt, at the southern tip of the island, where there is a huge floodlit field that's big enough for everyone – there's a massive stage at the far end and it's where everyone goes when we elect a new leader. Basil Herb walked onto the stage carrying a brown suitcase and made a speech about how he had built something that would provide all the electricity we would need forever. We all cheered and shouted, "Ba-sil, Ba-sil, Ba-sil, Ba-sil" for a long time. Basil opened his suitcase and took out some sort of control panel. He pressed a big red button and a section of the ground slid slowly open. Very gradually and with a lot of strange grinding sounds, something started to rise from out of an enormous pit that must have been dug right next to the underground factory. After forty minutes we all saw the full height and width of the world's biggest wind turbine. Basil explained that, with a total height of 306 metres and with 126-metre blades, the turbine would generate free electricity forever.

Gerald: Wonderful news! You must be so grateful to have free energy, and Mr Herb will be your island's hero.

Lollipop: Sadly not. The very light breeze could not turn the blades at all, and no electricity has been generated by the turbine, which was lowered back into its underground pit and has stayed there. Basil Herb tried his best but failed.

Gerald: Have you tried other ways to generate electricity?

Lollipop: Basil had spent more than half of his fortune on the wind turbine, but he was still a very very very very very very very very very very very very very very very very very very very rich man and he spent more of his money on creating floating turbines that, he insisted, would generate electricity from the power of the waves. Ocean wave energy can be converted into electrical energy by harnessing the up-and-down motion of ocean waves. Unfortunately, the up-and-down motion of waves simply doesn't happen around Silly Island, and the turbines failed. Basil Herb later tried to tell us about something called solar power, but by then we had had enough of his strange ideas and ignored him.

Gerald: That's very sad news. If you have almost run out of coal and can't find ways to use wind or wave power, will you all have to leave the island?

Lollipop: I wish you hadn't asked me that question, Colin. When anything starts to make us feel sad, we must become silly in order to get our happiness back. So, as soon as this interview ends, I will walk backwards, saying the alphabet backwards across the shallow end of the swimming pool in Dimble. After that I will paint the tip of my nose bright silver and sing silly songs for six hours. Then I might feel better again.

Gerald: I'm so sorry to have upset you. Just one final question – how did you become leader of Silly Island?

Lollipop: Anyone who would like to be leader has to explain what they would do to make Silly Island an even sillier and therefore happier place. My plan listed five promises: firstly, to introduce an outdoor Silly Show at 5.12 pm every Hippetyscringeday, with silly songs, dances and jokes presented by anyone at all; secondly, to invite an expert in juggling into schools, in order to teach all children to juggle silly objects of their choice: thirdly, to appoint a shouting person to go round the island on a bicycle shouting the news with a silly voice, thereby using less electricity; fourthly, to give sugar-free fruit jelly* to anyone who wants it; and finally, to rewrite our dictionary by including new words that islanders might invent. People must have liked my promises because most of them voted for me. I'm really looking forward to the next five years.

Gerald: I'm glad to hear it. You have a lot of work to do – I hope you have a lot of people to support you.

---

* The Silly Islanders have their own special recipe for sugar-free fruit jelly made with vegan gelatine, without additives or colouring and packed with enormous amounts of real fruit.

Lollipop: I do, I do, I do, I do. Do you? Yes, I do. The five other people who wanted to be leader but didn't receive as many votes as little me automatically became my assistants. Hippety-hooray for them.

Gerald: Lollipop, I'm sure you will have a lot to do now, especially because tomorrow will be your first Hippetyscringeday since becoming leader. It has been a pleasure to talk to you. Thank you for your time.

Lollipop: It was lovely to talk to you both. Be silly, Gerald, and may you never turn into a prickly cactus – unless you want to.

2. Almost Five Years Later

Lollipop McNoodly-Noodly's time as leader of Silly Island was almost at an end. She had been a popular leader and had introduced some very successful initiatives that pleased the people.

As promised, Lollipop organised outdoor Silly Shows, and they continue to take place in Sillytown Sillystadium at 5.12 pm every Hippetyscringeday. She is assisted by her twelve-year-old son Jazz, who had proved to be an accomplished rhubarb juggler. He is one of the many young jugglers who learned the art thanks to expert teaching in the island's schools. Mr Bottle, the juggling teacher, does his job well, although some parents are concerned that more time in school seems to be spent on juggling than on other silly activities such as standing on one leg in buckets of home-made slime and winking at trees.

Each Silly Show lasts for precisely one hour and twelve seconds and there are always plenty of acts to amuse and please the packed audiences. Lollipop introduces each act and Jazz helps to get the performers on and off stage quickly but safely. Some of the more popular acts are: The Invisible Crow (always the same routine but guaranteed to be invisible throughout); Happyjon Umbrella-Zup the upside-down dancer; Phil, Phil, Bob, Phil, Phil and Phil the whistling statues; Zenda the Wiggly; Holly the Human Tree; and Jazz himself. Over the five years that Lollipop and Jazz have organised the shows there has been just one unfortunate incident, that being when the invisible crow went missing until it revealed itself foolishly trying to stop Zenda the Wiggly from wiggling: Zenda and the crow are now good friends.

Just as she had promised, Lollipop appointed a shouting person to go round the island on a bicycle, shouting the news with a silly voice. The advertisement for the vacant position had attracted much interest and Lollipop had held auditions on the beach at Beachy Bay. Those applying for this important position were told that three things were needed if they were to be considered for the post: firstly, a working bicycle was essential; secondly, a loud, clear voice was obviously important; and thirdly, that voice needed to be as silly as possible. Many of those who applied for the job could certainly shout loudly in a silly voice, for that was something to which Silly Islanders were accustomed, but very few people had a working bicycle. There were silly bicycles, of course, such as those with square wheels, some that were fitted with stabilisers for very young children and even one with hundreds of bells. After an afternoon of great hilarity Lollipop chose Phil de Bucket (the second Phil in Phil, Phil, Bob, Phil, Phil and Phil the whistling statues) because, although his bicycle had no working bell, he could whistle loudly to let people know he was about to shout at the top of his voice. Phil loved his job, and his wide range of silly voices was loved by all.

Lollipop had promised to give free fruit jelly to anyone who wanted it, but she could not have been prepared for the demands placed upon her by the fruit-loving islanders, who wanted their favourite jelly at any time of day or night. It was obvious that a huge operation needed to be established. Because the coal mine was running out of coal, many of the miners were losing their jobs, so Lollipop gave them work making and serving fruit jelly in five centres across the island as well as running 'jellymobile' delivery services for those in urgent need. Many flavours of sugar-free fruit jelly are now produced, providing islanders with a choice of raspberry, orange, blackberry, lime, strawberry or many other fruits. Deliveries to one particular customer can be quite hazardous: those taking jellies to Zenda the Wiggly are advised to wear additional protective clothing during the handover of the items.

True to her word, Lollipop has rewritten the island's dictionary by including new words that residents have invented. A total of one hundred and seventy words have been accepted and, of those, the following are now commonly heard in everyday discussion:

blanketeer – a person who always asks for an extra blanket for their sleeping cat

giddling – wearing shoes, boots, trainers or wellies on the wrong feet (eg "I see you are giddling again today, Mrs Postcard")

J sharp – a wrong note in music (eg "I played a J sharp by mistake")

hoohoy – a friendly word to use when meeting someone for the first time, said while touching one's right ear with the tip of one's left little finger

Mister Porridge – a recently discovered tiny mammal with long brown fur - it can run faster than an athlete, so has never been caught

quigglesnout – a nose that has a wobbly bit at the end

quoo – a very long queue, especially when trying to get a good seat at Silly Shows

splinge – the sound made by a cow when laughing at its own jokes

shiddle – an uncomfortable way of walking and giggling at the same time, caused by an itch in that bit between the shoulder blades that you just can't reach, however hard you try

thith – a boggy area of land with paving stones across it, making a strange bubbly sound as the mud moves beneath the stones under your weight

zim – something to say while standing on one leg for longer than six hours

Two very interesting words were invented by a very old man called Norman Conquest, who lives in Purple, a small village in the east of the island, and they are:

bandurple – a gentleman's hat, made by knitting reeds

gurple – a five-wheeled bicycle, invented by N Conquest

Norman's ambition was to write a limerick beginning *There was an old man from Purple.* After many years of trying, Norman came to the conclusion that nothing rhymes with 'Purple', so he decided to invent two new words in order to complete his limerick -

There was an old man from Purple
Who made a bright green bandurple
He wore it each day
At work and at play
And sometimes while riding his gurple.

Before Norman's words could be accepted into the dictionary, he had to prove that there were such things as bandurples and gurples. It was a very proud day for Norman when, wearing his bandurple, he appeared on stage at a Silly Show and recited his limerick to a delighted crowd before drawing back a curtain to reveal his gurple for the first time. The crowd roared their approval, giving Norman a standing ovation as he rode the gurple beyond the stage, away from the show and down the road, only to lose control at the very first bend and topple slowly into a duck pond. He was heard to shout, "Oh zurple!" very loudly, which led to him receiving a warning for bad language, this being the first time such a dreadful word had ever been used on the island. Although Norman's gurple was the first and last of its kind, it was eventually rebuilt and taken to *Silly Old Things*, the island's museum, where it has pride of place and is labelled *Gurple – very dangerously silly*. Happily for Norman Conquest, the bandurple was loved by many, and he now teaches the art of reed knitting at Purple School, where the skilful children can produce up to ten bandurples each week in order to meet the growing demand.*

After five successfully silly years, Lollipop's term as leader of the island was coming to an end. She felt a lot of satisfaction in what she and her assistants had achieved. However, she knew that whoever took over from her would have to seriously address the most important issue facing the future of the island and its people – how to find ways of generating electricity before the coal mine finally had to close. Sadly, Lollipop had not addressed this problem, mainly because the people didn't like talking about unhappy things but also because she simply kept putting it off 'until another day.'

With just five weeks to go before the election for new leader was to take place, Lollipop chaired what was supposed to be her final meeting of the island cowsill (what we usually call a council). The cowsill, consisting of Lollipop and her five assistants, had a meeting every forty-eight days.

*If you wish to order a bandurple please send a drawing of an enormous fruit jelly monster to Norman Conquest, False Beard Cottage, Purple, Silly Island. You won't receive a bandurple unless you live on Silly Island, but there's no harm in trying (or is there?)

3. The Cowsill Meeting

As was the custom, the final meeting of Lollipop's island cowsill took place in her kitchen, with refreshments provided and served by Lollipop's husband, Tim-Tom McNoodly-Noodly. The cowsill members arrived one by one and each in turn knocked on Lollipop and Tim-Tom's front door. Tim-Tom refused to let them enter until they told him a joke that would make him laugh.

First to knock was Carol Christmas, who loved telling jokes. However, hers were always dreadful jokes that very few people could understand. Quite frankly, the islanders were fed up with trying to understand Carol's jokes and just laughed at them to make her feel happy.

"Tell me a good joke to make me laugh," requested Tim-Tom.

"Knock knock," replied Carol, already starting to giggle at her own joke.

"Who's there?"

"Carol."

"Carol who?" Tim-Tom was beginning to feel a little weary of her jokes and suspected that he was going to hear the words, "Carol Christmas", to which he would have to laugh loud and long. But he was wrong.

"Carol, Carol, sitting in a barrel!" Carol immediately exploded with laughter and Tim-Tom forced himself to join in as he opened the door. There was Carol and, joy of joys, she was indeed sitting in a barrel.

Tim-Tom was delighted with the unique experience of a genuinely funny joke from Carol. He joined in the fun she had created by saying, "Oh Carol, you are a barrel of laughs!"

There was an uncomfortable silence. "Was that supposed to be funny?" asked Carol, climbing out of the barrel and entering the house.

The second assistant to arrive was fifteen-year-old Leighton Early who, of course, had been just ten when he stood for election. He knocked firmly on the door.

"Tell me a joke, please."

"I was on television for three weeks before I noticed that I had an armchair."

"Leighton, that's a dreadful joke, but worthy of going into next year's Christmas crackers, so I'll let you in."

"Thanks, T-T McN-N." Tim-Tom greeted Leighton and, as he closed the door, he realised that another member of the cowsill was just arriving. A gentle knock indicated the arrival of Mrs February April, a Sillytown school teacher.

"Tell me a good joke, please."

"There was a young fellow named Rod
Who didn't like haddock or cod
He liked eating chips
With soft-boiled egg dips
While giving his head a good nod."

"Very inventive, February! Come on in, please."

"I was rather pleased with that one myself," admitted Mrs April. She marched swiftly past Tim-Tom and shook hands with her assembled colleagues.

Leighton, who had once been taught by February, knew he should feel easy in her company but always worried that she might remember the day he had sat on another child's bandurple, causing the maker to burst into tears when the rest of the class had thought they were doing the right thing by laughing.

There was another knock, and Tim-Tom asked the unseen visitor to tell him a joke.

"What is the difference between a dish containing fruit and large white arctic mammals?"

Tim-Tom had heard a lot of *what is the difference between* jokes but this one was new to him. "I don't know; please tell me the difference between a dish containing fruit and large white arctic mammals."

"One is a bowl of pears, and the others are polar bears."

Tim-Tim's reaction to the joke was to take a couple of seconds to think about what the answer meant before bursting out laughing as he opened the door to greet a delighted 88-year-old Jim Nasium, a former coal miner, now retired. Tim-Tom was still laughing a minute later as he closed the door just before the final member of the cowsill arrived. Hughie Budge had been manager of the Dimble coal mine for the past six years and was also a part-time wrestler, specialising in wrestling against himself. Hughie had wrestled himself twenty-seven times, winning thirteen, losing thirteen and controversially drawing one when he complained of a headache in his big toe.

"Do you have a joke for me?" asked Tim-Tom.

The response genuinely worried Tim-Tom because Hughie's voice sounded so weak, being a quiet mixture of words and animal sounds. "I… *neigh*… can't… *neigh*… speak… *neigh*… very… *neigh*… well… *neigh*," spluttered Hughie. Tim-Tom decided that Hughie must be unwell and opened the door immediately. Hughie had a big grin on his face as he explained, "I'm a little hoarse today!"

Five minutes later Tim-Tom revealed some delicious home-baked cakes and six large mugs of his own mushroom and coltsfoot tea for the cowsill to enjoy throughout the meeting, and he then went through to the living room to watch his favourite television programme, Sillynation Street.

Eventually, Lollipop called the meeting to order and passed round copies of the Splop (what we call Agenda) for the meeting.

SILLY ISLAND COWSILL MEETING 43rd July
SPLOP

1 Refreshments
2 Silly Shows
3 Juggling lessons
4 News-shouting person
5 Sugar-free fruit jelly update
6 Dictionary – new words
8 Anything else (silly)
9 Anything else (not silly, if we really must)
10 Refreshments

Splop Items 1 and 2 took almost an hour because Tim-Tom had provided such wonderful refreshments for the final cowsill meeting. The third item, 'Silly Shows', involved many congratulations to Lollipop for organising such fun for everyone. Jim Nasium asked Lollipop if she and Jazz would consider continuing to lead the weekly shows after the election, to which Lollipop replied, "We would love to carry on forever and ever and ever and ever and ever and ever and ever and ever. Thank you dingle-dangly much for asking."

There was also agreement that the juggling lessons were a great success, but February felt that adults were missing out on the chance to learn from the great Mr Bottle. Leighton, who had qualified as a Grade 72 juggler, said that he would be happy to help Mr Bottle run evening classes for adults, and all agreed that they should be arranged as soon as possible. Carol added that she hoped it would be possible to also hold synchronised winking at trees classes during the winter months, but Lollipop suggested that interest in the activity was on the wane. "Well then," replied Carol, "we should make an effort to re-wink the population. The old ways shouldn't be allowed to cookie-crumble into the distant past."

To everyone's delight, Leighton revealed that he had sometimes seen Mr Bottle winking at the same time as juggling, and suggested, "If we can all learn to wink while facing trees as we juggle we could then try to phase out the juggling part of the activity while continuing to wink." Leighton's brilliant idea caused much delight among the cowsill members.

News-shouting was also discussed, and all agreed that Phil de Bucket should be asked if he would continue in his important role. Lollipop felt certain he would, but added, "We must help Phil to look after his voice. All that shouting can't be good for him. I suggest that we give him a ventriloquist's dummy to do the speaking for him when he isn't shouting."

Hughie revealed that he had once tried to be a ventriloquist, and had a dummy rabbit called Reginald that he didn't use any more, simply because he found Reginald to be quite argumentative. He said he was "more than happipipipy" to give Reginald to Phil.

Free fruit jelly was now an accepted and much-needed part of everyday life on Silly Island. The demand for jelly was not at all wobbly, and the production and delivery worked very well. Lollipop carefully read out a letter she had received from

Zenda the Wiggly, 'carefully' because the writing was very difficult to read, being as wiggly as a wiggliest thing you can imagine. Zenda agreed that the delivery workers needed to wear protective clothing when they brought her jellies but asked if she could be provided with the same sort of protection herself. Leighton suggested that Zenda should simply stop wiggling during the delivery and while eating her jellies. Lollipop decided that, in her reply to Zenda, she would request that wiggling during her performance in Silly Shows was all that was required, and that no wiggling should take place at other times, particularly during jelly deliveries.

After the second hour of the meeting, Tim-Tom, holding a teapot, popped his head round the door and quietly asked, "Are you ready for more scrimmety-scrummeties yet or should I come back later?" Lollipop decided that the meeting had been going on for such a long time that they should simply pass round the Silly Dictionary, containing its many new words, while they ate and drank. This would mean having an excuse to hold another 'final' meeting a few days later to discuss Splop items 8 and 9, and so it was agreed.

Hughie said, "You are all welcome to come to my house on Wednesday if you like. The football should have arrived by then, so we can practise."

"Practise what? Juggling or winking at trees?" asked February.

"No, I mean practise footballing. Don't forget, we're playing Brazil next week." They all burst out laughing, except Hughie, who suddenly remembered there was something very important he had forgotten to tell the others. He silently slumped back into his chair, embarrassed at his own foolishness.

But Hughie wasn't the only one who hadn't raised something of importance to them all. Lollipop knew that, as usual, she had failed to confront the single most important problem facing the future of Silly Island – that their only means for providing electricity was to use coal, and that the mine would have to close very soon.

4. School Report

When eleven-year-old Spring Herb arrived home from school she was feeling quite anxious. In her bag was her school report. Children on Silly Island usually look forward to reading their school reports, because their teachers give them a lot of praise for being creatively silly as well as for their general learning and effort. But Spring wasn't like many of the other children in some ways. The granddaughter of the once very very very very very very very very very very very very very very very very very very very very very very very very very very very very very very very very very very very very very very very very very very very very very very very very very very very very very very very very very very very very very very very very very very very very very very very very very very very very rich Basil Herb, her family had lived near a small town called Crunch since arriving on Silly Island eight years ago, but she still sometimes felt like an outsider. The other children were lovely, and she had many close friends, but Spring had a desire to be taken seriously rather than silly a lot of the time. She worried that her school report might contain comments such as 'must try not to be so serious', 'should show her silly side more often' or 'not interested in important activities like flannel throwing.'

Spring lived with her parents Rosemary Herb and Woody Herb and her four-year-old brother Herbie, next door to Basil, her famous grandfather. Rosemary and Woody supported Spring in her desire to conform to the silliness that was experienced on a day-to-day basis, but they felt the same unease as their daughter, having lived in Western Europe for most of their lives. Both parents liked the fact that they had to be sensible in their work, Rosemary as one of the Silly Island's doctors and Woody as captain and pilot of 'The Fly', the island's one aeroplane. This meant that they only really needed to be silly when not at work, which helped them greatly. Needless to say, Herbie, who was born on the island, was already extremely silly.

"Did you have a good day at school, Spring?" asked Woody when they met in the kitchen.

"Oh Dad, it was really silly all day."

"I guess you have mixed feelings about it, then."

"I do, Dad, and I got my school report today."

"Well, let's go through to the living room and open it, shall we? Mum and Grandfather are there having a cup of tea with a treacle and cabbage bar each."

"Why can't we go back to having tea and biscuits like we used to?"

"You can have biscuits any time you like. We're only having treacle and cabbage bars as a trial. To be honest, they really are as horrible as you would expect." They both laughed.

Rosemary and Basil smiled when they saw Spring come through to join them, but Rosemary could immediately tell that something was bothering her daughter. "Hello, love. How's things?"

"Here's my school report," replied Spring, coming straight to the point.

"Lovely! Let's have a look at the good news." Spring cautiously handed over the envelope to her mother. Woody sat in his special armchair, and

Spring remained standing, feeling apprehensive about what her parents would say when they had read the report.

A few awkward minutes passed before Rosemary proclaimed, "It's a great report, as I expected."

"It can't be – I'm just not silly enough."

"Don't tell your friends, love, but some things are more important than silliness. Your teachers know you well, and they recognise your many talents."

As Rosemary was speaking, Spring noticed that Basil was having a sneaky peep at the report. Then a grin appeared on her grandfather's face, and he suddenly leapt into the air, throwing his arms above his head as he shouted, "Yes, yes, yes!"

"Calm down, Father," gasped a concerned Woody. "Do you need one of your pink tablets?"

"No, I do not. All I need is my wonderful granddaughter!"

Spring had no idea what could have caused Basil to behave in this way, and she quietly asked,

"You already have me, Grandfather, I'm here. What do you want me to do?"

The great man was beside himself with glee as he sat down and started to explain. "Spring, your school report for art and design says, 'Spring is the most talented young artist I have ever had the pleasure to teach. Her huge paintings are full of colour and fun and I'm sure she has a great future in this subject.' Do you know what that tells me? It means that not only are you good at silly subjects, but also in one special subject where you don't have to be silly at all, and your teacher has declared that you are the very best."

"I'm sure Mr Acrylic is exaggerating, Grandfather."

"Well, I don't think he is. Let me tell you something." All the family could tell by the tone of Basil's voice that he wanted them to sit quietly and listen to what he was going to say. "When I was your age a lot of the other people in my class used to be quite naughty in class. They talked too much about things that were not really important, like television gossip and who was the strongest, fastest or most handsome. At playtimes they only wanted to play chasing games, ball games or pretend fights. I wasn't like them. I wanted to learn, to study and to invent. I told the headteacher about it and she arranged for me to have extra lessons with her uncle, who was an engineer. I went to see him in his garden workshop four times a week and he taught me lots of things about how to solve problems by using my brain. After a month or so he told me that I was the best learner he had ever met, and he encouraged me to become an engineer. I worked very hard and eventually got a place at a great university, from where I graduated with first-class honours."

"Why are you telling me this, Grandfather?" Spring didn't immediately understand what her grandfather's past had to do with her school report.

"I'm getting to that bit, Spring," Basil said, reassuringly. "Bear with me, please. It was thanks to the skill and enthusiasm of my headteacher and her uncle that I fulfilled my dream to become an engineer and, as you know, I set up a business that grew to become a world leader in environmental engineering and technology." He paused, looked directly at Spring and smiled. "You are very much like me, Spring. You have a special talent that has been recognised by someone. My talent was in engineering, but yours is in art, producing huge, colourful paintings. I suspected as much when I saw the painting on your bedroom ceiling."

"You mean when you sometimes told me bedtime stories about the flying bed? You never mentioned my ceiling painting then."

"That's because I never considered that it could have been painted by you. At first, I thought it was actually a photograph of the family. In that very special painting, our faces are so full of life and fun. How long did it take you to paint it all?"

Spring thought for a moment, before saying, "I painted it just before I had my daily shower after our evening meals but before bedtime, and I probably finished it in about a week."

"My my, that's astonishing!" Her grandfather's smile was wider than ever, and tears of happiness were rolling down his cheeks. Rosemary and Woody were holding hands, so proud of their daughter and not wanting to interrupt the lovely words they were hearing about her.

Basil's expression suddenly changed, and his serious, thoughtful but slightly mischievous expression suggested that he was about to say something profound. "My dear Spring, you are going to become the next leader of Silly Island!" There was a lengthy silence.

Eventually, Woody spoke. "But Basil, you have just reminded us that Spring's talent is for her wonderful painting. You know just as well as us that the leader of Silly Island must have a completely different skill set. Lollipop McNoodly-Noodly has been a wonderful leader for the past five years - she can organise others, she has management skills and people love her crazy approach to life. Lollipop has a weakness, though - oh yes, she certainly knows how to help people to be happy by being silly, but she fails to address the fact that there is virtually no coal left in the mine. She is in denial, and the new leader will probably feel the same way and continue to concentrate on silly policies."

"And in any case, Grandfather," objected Spring, "I don't want to be the leader of Silly Island. I'm just not silly. It wouldn't work. I would fail, just like..." She stopped abruptly, but Basil knew what she was going to say.

"Just like me? Oh yes, I failed... I failed in a big way, didn't I? But my plans for providing green energy for the island failed because I had no support. The people still think I'm a failure, but the big difference for you is that you will be supported not only by me but also by my great friend and brilliant artist Dr Alessandra Cafasso, who will be coming here from Rome next week, to stay with us for a few days."

Spring, Woody and Rosemary sat open-mouthed, but for different reasons. Spring had now lost all understanding of what her grandfather meant, but her parents knew that Dr Alessandra Cafasso was one of the most famous and inspirational women in the world. However, none of them could have imagined what was going to happen when Dr Cafasso and Spring got together.

And then young Herbie came bounding into the room, shouting, "I've been in the middle of the garden, standing on top of a stool and singing *Shoo, shoo my shoe* for the past thirty minutes. That was really silly!"

5. A Chance Meeting

Spring was sitting in front of the television the following morning, but she wasn't really taking any notice of whatever programme was on. She was still thinking about her school report and trying to make sense of her grandfather's extraordinary reaction to finding out about her artistic talent. She thought her drawings and paintings were mostly quite good but had no idea that Basil was going to suggest that her painting skills could somehow prepare her for being the next leader of Silly Island. She also wondered what the mysterious Dr Alessandra Cafasso could have to do with anything that was going on in her life, although she was aware that her grandfather had some incredibly famous friends. He had never wanted her to meet any of them before, though. How intriguing!

"Spring, are you ready?" Rosemary was calling.

"Ready for what, Mum?"

"Have you forgotten? We're going to Sillytown to look for a birthday present for Herbie." Spring jumped up, switched off the television and followed

Rosemary to the car. The family had very few ideas about what Herbie would like for his birthday, and most of the toy shops seemed to be full of ridiculously trivial things as far as Spring was concerned. Why couldn't Silly Islanders realise that not everything has to be silly?

Twenty minutes later they were in town, in the middle of the biggest toy shop, and Rosemary was looking seriously at a construction set containing various metal rods, wheels, screws, some kind of square metal plates, a screwdriver and a book of ideas. "What do you think about us getting him this, Spring?"

Spring thought her mother's suggestion was a very good one and added, "It's great, Mum. Herbie could learn a lot about engineering by playing with it, so Grandfather would be pleased with the choice. But he seems to be like the rest of the children of his age."

"What do you mean?"

"He just seems to want toys that make funny noises, or that crash into other things, or that annoy grown-ups and…" She hesitated.

"And big sisters, is that what you were going to say?" They both laughed, and then decided it was time to give Herbie what they wanted him to have rather than to ask him if he wanted yet another whoopee cushion.

As they were leaving the shop with the chosen gift, Rosemary suddenly received a text message that changed her plans. Her friend Byjingo lived near the centre of Sillytown and was texting to ask Rosemary if she would like to call for a buttercup coffee before she went home. Rosemary was always happy to meet her friend and asked Spring, "Would you like to come with me? We'll probably be there for about an hour."

Spring's mind was still full of thoughts about her grandfather's enthusiasm towards her and how she was going to tell him that she simply didn't want to be leader of Silly Island, so she asked, "Would it be all right if I have a walk round town and meet you back at the car in an hour?"

"That's fine, Spring. Just phone me if you change your mind and would like to join us."

Still feeling rather confused, Spring wandered away from the centre of Sillytown and into an area of housing she had never visited before. After passing a small corner shop that seemed to be selling everything from paper shoes to dusters designed to add dust to furniture, she heard a distant rhythmic drumming sound and a voice that seemed to be singing about a duck-billed platypus. Spring felt as if the sounds were beckoning her to move closer, and she soon found herself outside an open window from which came the unmistakable sound of a drum kit and someone singing a chorus,

"Oh, duck-billed platypus, please stay here with us
Here on Silly Island when it's raining orange juice
You can stay all day, and then sleep in the hay
Alongside Bertie Buffalo and crazy Monty Moose."

When the chorus was repeated, Spring found herself joining in, and she had just got to the bit about sleeping in the hay when the drumming stopped and a boy's smiling face appeared at the open window. "Hello, who are you?"

Spring suddenly felt self-conscious and realised she was actually being quite rude by listening at someone's open window and, even worse, by joining in with their singing. "Oh, sorry. I'm Spring."

"Hi Spring, I'm Jazz McNoodly-Noodly." Spring suddenly realised that the boy was none other than the son of Lollipop McNoodly-Noodly, the island's leader. She recognised him as the chap who cleverly juggled rhubarb at the Silly Shows on Hippetyscringedays. Despite her view that much of what took place on the island was too ridiculous to be remotely interesting, she loved sitting on the front row at the Hippetyscringeday Shows and was fascinated by the energy and skill of the young rhubarb juggler with whom she had just come face-to-face.

Somewhat starstruck, Spring knew what she wanted to say and came straight out with, "I love your rhubarb juggling, Jazz, and you're a great drummer too!"

"Oh gee, thanks," chirped Jazz, adding, "Aren't you the one in the front row who claps loudest when I juggle?"

"Do I? Oh, I suppose I might be!"

To Spring's great surprise, Jazz suddenly jumped through the window and joined her on the pavement outside his house. "Come on," he said, "I'll teach you how to juggle. Follow me," and he led her round to the back of the house, where he pointed to an enormous patch of rhubarb. "Help yourself, Spring. You can take some home to practise with if you like."

"Thanks, but I think it might be better if I started juggling with something a bit easier than rhubarb!"

A few moments later, after Jazz had shown Spring a few simple techniques using soft balls, the two of them were juggling together. As the minutes passed, Spring learned more and more moves, and Jazz told her she had a lot of natural talent. Realising that it was almost time for her to meet her mum, Spring thanked Jazz for showing her how to juggle and explained that she had to leave. As she turned away, Jazz suddenly asked, "Would you like to juggle with me at tomorrow's Hippetyscringeday Silly Show?"

Spring was dumbfounded but excited. "Do you think I'm good enough?"

"Of course, and I really want you to do it! Meet me half an hour before the show starts and we'll have another practise."

"Wow – thank you so much! I'll be there." Her mind in a whirl of happiness, excitement and disbelief at what had just happened, Spring ran back to the car, arriving just as her mother returned.

"Did you find something to pass the time?" asked Rosemary.

"Did I? You bet!" replied Spring. "I'll tell you all about it on the way home." A short time later they arrived home and, as they got out of the car, they were both singing a song together for the first time,

"Oh, duck-billed platypus, please stay here with us
Here on Silly Island when it's raining orange juice

You can stay all day, and then sleep in the hay
Alongside Bertie Buffalo and crazy Monty Moose."

6. Hughie's Big News

SILLY ISLAND COWSILL MEETING 45ᵗʰ July SPLOP

1 Refreshments
2 Anything else (silly)
3 Anything else (not silly, if we really must)
4 Refreshments

Wednesday evening's continuation of the final cowsill meeting was the first to be held at Hughie Budge's home. Hughie was feeling nervous about the meeting, and he had completely forgotten that it was usual to ask cowsill members to tell a joke before allowing them to enter.

One by one, the members arrived at Hughie's house on time. Each knocked and waited but received no response, and when Jim Nasium got there he found all the others waiting by the door, telling their jokes to each other.

"Hello, Jim," said Lollipop, "I don't suppose you know where Hughie is, do you?"

"No," he replied, adding, "Could he be hiding up there?" They all looked towards the nearest tree, which grew at the side of Hughie's lawn.

"Perhaps he's behind the tree," suggested Carol.

"Or inside it?" muttered Leighton.

"Yes, maybe that's not a real tree. Could it be Hughie in a fantastic disguise?" wondered February.

Moving away from tree theories, Lollipop had the idea that Hughie might have started playing a game of hide and seek. Because it would be wrong for them to go into the house without his permission, they decided to go round the side of the house and search for Hughie in the back garden.

Finding Hughie didn't take long. Peeping round the side of the house, they all saw him sitting on a deck chair with his head in his hands.

"Whatever's the matter, Hughie?" asked a concerned February.

Hughie looked up at the smiling faces and muttered, "I have let you all down and I have forgotten to get any refreshments ready."

"Goodness me, that doesn't matter," said Lollipop, kindly. "We can enjoy fresh water instead."

"You don't seem to understand," mumbled Hughie. "I should have told everybody about the football match a long time ago."

"Surely, what you announced at the last meeting about playing a match against Brazil next week was a joke?" asked Jim. But Hughie's expression left them in no doubt that he had been telling the truth. He had simply forgotten to tell anyone that, many months ago, he had been contacted by the Brazilian Football Confederation, who offered to send their national team to Silly Island for a friendly match, and he had agreed to it.

There was a very long, awkward pause before Lollipop smiled once again, and said, "Hughie, you are a genius!" Hughie raised his eyebrows as he stared at Lollipop, wondering if she was being sarcastic. "What you have done is to forget to tell us you have organised a foot-thingy-whatsit match until it was almost too late. But, because of you, this event could go down in history as the silliest thing that has ever happened on Silly Island." Holding out her arms, Lollipop beckoned to them all, saying, "And now, cowsill members, please join me in three Silly Island cheers for Hughie. Hip hip...."

"Hippopotamus," they all yelled.

"Hip hip…"

"Hippopotamus."

"Hip hip..."

"Hippopotamus." A huge smile finally appeared on Hughie's face, as he joined in with the traditional Silly Island dance of celebration, where six left leg hops are followed by seven right leg hops, then two claps, four head nods and finally a star jump while shouting "Eeksie-peeksie."

"Now Hughie," went on Lollipop, "tell us all about this foot-thingy-whatsit, or whatever it is. The rest of the Splop will have to wait for another time."

Feeling much better after the three cheers, Hughie told the others what he should have explained some time ago. The Brazilian Football Confederation had asked if they could play an international match against Silly Island because they were preparing for next year's World Cup. They explained that the team wanted to try out some new tactics that they didn't want other teams to know about. They had been looking for a way of playing a match that would not attract publicity, and the opportunity to play on Silly Island was just what they had been looking for.

Of course, the cowsill members wanted to know much more. A lot of details needed to be properly discussed and, after another fifteen minutes, it had been decided that the match would be played the Saturday after next at Biggety-Big Beach, kicking-off at 2.22 pm. Lollipop said she would invite Gerald Grainger of UK21 Radio to commentate on the match through a microphone and loudspeaker provided by Mike R O'Phone, the island's electrician, so that all the people sitting on the sand dunes would know what was happening.

None of the cowsill members had ever played football before. This was not surprising because no-one on Silly Island had ever played football before, but Hughie explained that he had heard of the game and that his friend Woody Herb, who flew 'The Fly' to other parts of the world, believed it was quite popular in some countries.

Lollipop told them she would make sure that Phil de Bucket would shout out details of the match all over the island every day over the coming week so that everyone who wanted to watch the foot-thingy-whatsit could come and see what it was like.

Jim Nasium had something on his mind. With a rather worried expression, he asked Hughie, "Do you think the Brazil people know how to play football?" Hughie said he assumed they knew but, just to be on the safe side, he would pass a list of rules to the players before the match started.

The question of rules prompted Carol to ask, "Will you be passing the list of rules to our own players too?"

"Of course," replied Hughie.

Leighton asked Hughie who would be in the Silly Island team, to which Hughie replied, "I think we should all be in it, if you are all happy with that."

"That's a good idea," agreed February, adding, "but there are only six of us and, when I was teaching children about the history of shirts, I remember seeing a photograph of a football team wearing shirts which had numbers one to eleven on the players' backs."

His confidence growing, Hughie told them all that he would take responsibility for finding five other people who could play for the Silly Island team. "I'll stand on stage at the next Silly Show and ask for any volunteers to come forward," he said. "I can't imagine many people will be interested, but I'll try to explain that it might be good fun to play, and then see if anyone is prepared to give it a try."

Aware that the meeting had reached what seemed to be a suitable conclusion, Lollipop rounded things off by reminding the others that it would soon be time to organise the forthcoming election of new leader and cowsill for the next five years. They all agreed that the present cowsill should, as usual at these important times, interview candidates to hear what plans they would like to put forward to the people. Leighton felt that it might also be a good idea to organise a competitive silly event for the candidates to take part in, "Something like our own version of the Olympic Games," he explained.

"A wonderful idea," agreed Lollipop. "I propose that Leighton should take charge of organising the Sillylympics, and that the candidates will all take part in five events that will test their silliness as well as their leadership qualities." There was general agreement that the Sillylympics should take place soon after the candidates' interviews. The plans of the candidates and the results of the games could then be passed on to all islanders before they voted for their new leader at the special election meeting.

Hughie, now restored to being his usual happy self, stood up and shouted, "So now, everyone, please join me with three Silly Island cheers for our exciting Sillylympics! Hip hip...."

"Hippopotamus,"

"Hip hip…"

"Hippopotamus."

"Hip hip..."

"Hippopotamus."

The three cheers were just as loud and positive as they had been earlier in the meeting. Everyone immediately produced six left leg hops, then seven right leg hops followed by two claps, four head nods and a star jump while shouting "Eeksie-peeksie."

7. The Telephone Call

Jill (Secretary): Good morning. Welcome to UK21 Radio. My name is Jill. How may I help you?

Lollipop: Goodeth morningeth, Jill. My name is Lollipop McNoodly-Noodly. You may help me by gluing a frog licence into your frog licence album if you like, or you may help by permitting me to speak to Gerald Grainger.

Jill: Are you trying to be funny or something?

Lollipop: I suppose my answer to your question must be 'something', as I'm not trying to be funny. However, it is in my nature to help you to smile rather than to frown, and to smile properly you need to exercise your smiley muscles.

Jill: So, what's all this about frog licences?

Lollipop: Here on Silly Island we insist that all frogs are treated with kindness and consideration. Anyone wishing to adopt a frog must have a licence to show their respect and understanding towards their little green friend.

Jill: Ah, now I see! Mr Grainger has told me all about Silly Island. He loved speaking to you a few years ago, and often wonders if he will have another opportunity to do so again.

Lollipop: Yippety doodle! I would like to speak to him too, so both our dreams can come true. By the way, what is your dream that you would like to come true?

Jill: I would very much like to have met William the Conqueror. I researched the Battle of Hastings as part of my university course, and I discovered that William had four sons and five daughters. My dream is that I'm one of his daughters, a kind-hearted princess who is a friend to all I meet.

Lollipop: Then I'm sorry to have to tell you that I cannot make your dream come true because time travel is not possible, even on Silly Island. However, I could send you a frog licence if you wish.

Jill: Why would I need a frog licence?

Lollipop: I have heard a story about a princess who kissed a frog and turned him into a prince. It's a good idea to remind princesses that they should not kiss frogs, even in their dreams. If kissed, a frog can display an elevated sense of importance, and we wouldn't want frogs to go round ordering people to clean their shoes for them, would we?

Jill: I would be delighted and honoured to receive a Silly Island frog licence. Thank you very much. Mr Grainger is in the next room – I'll let him know you are on the line.

Lollipop: Thank you, Jill. By the way, if you dream about that conqueror chap again, please tell him that he might be good at playing with conkers, but he should be careful not to use them as weapons in battles - he could easily zonk some poor king in the eye if he's not careful!

Jill: Thank you for the advice, Mrs McNoodly-Noodly. I'm now handing you over to Mr Grainger.

Gerald Grainger: Hello, Lollipop. It's very good to speak to you again. How are you?

Lollipop: I'm full of honey-flavoured wheelbarrows. Are you also well, Doreen?

Gerald: I'm very happy to hear your voice and, by the way, I'm still called Gerald. What can I do for you?

Lollipop: I have contacted you to ask if you would care to do me a very big favour. But before I tell you what it is, I must ask you to promise not to tell anyone about our discussion.

Gerald: I'm intrigued! Very well, you have my word that I will not reveal our conversation to anyone.

Lollipop: Thank you. Please repeat after me: I agree not to tell any person, tree, animal, plant, wheelbarrow or fish about my discussion with Lollipop McNoodly-Noodly.

Gerald: I agree not to tell any person, tree, animal, plant, wheelbarrow or fish about my discussion with Lollipop McNoodly-Noodly.

Lollipop: I'll come straight to the point. On the Saturday of next week a Silly Island team will be playing Brazil in a game of foot-thingy-whatsit. The game isn't really called that, but I can't remember its real name.

Gerald: Brazil are famous for playing football, but I don't suppose….

Lollipop: Football - oh yes, that's it. Anyway, I wondered if you….

Gerald: I assume you are being silly because there's no way that Silly Island could compete with Brazil at football.

Lollipop: Me, being silly? Oh no, I'm being very serious. Anyway, I wondered if you would be so kind as to come along to Silly Island and commentate on the game for us. It is being held on the sand at Biggity-Big Beach at 2.22pm and I imagine that a lot of Silly Islanders will come to watch. We don't know anything about foot-thingy-whatsit, and I hope you can help by speaking through a microphone and loudspeaker so that all the people sitting on the sand dunes will understand what is taking place.

Gerald: It would be wonderful to visit Silly Island and I would be absolutely delighted to do that for you, but how would I get there and back?

Lollipop: Oh goodety-good! Our pilot, Woody Herb, can pick you up from wherever you choose and bring you to Sillytown Hairport. From there you will be asked to ride on a tandem, sitting behind my friend Phil de Bucket, to the beach. After the game you will be able to meet all the players and join us all in a barber-queue on the beach. You will return to the hairport with Phil, and then Woody will fly you home. Are you happity-hapstoat with those arrangements?

Gerald: You bet I am! Can I ask why this is all to be kept secret?

Lollipop: The Brazilians don't want anyone else to know about the game because they are trying out their ideas in preparation for the next foot-thingy-whatsit World Cup. If you were to ever tell anyone about it you would have to be squirted by a thousand water pistols.

Gerald: I see, but…. Lollipop, if the people of Silly Island don't know anything about football how are you going to stand any chance at all in the match?

Lollipop: I don't think that matters too much, does it? We'll just enjoy ourselves. For the first part of the game we'll simply sit down and watch Brazil play, and then we'll know what to do.

Gerald: This is all so incredible. I hope you realise what you are letting yourselves in for.

Lollipop: Don't worry, Mr Bumblebop, we are used to playing games, in fact, we are very good at some of them, like Hunt the Saucer, Staring at Wood and Throwing Flannels, so foot-thingy-whatsit should be no problem.

Gerald: What colour shirts will your team be wearing?

Lollipop: I think we'll leave it to each player to choose for themselves. I will be wearing a stupendous flowery dress.

Gerald: The Brazil team will all be wearing the same colour shirts with their names and numbers on the back. When I am commentating, how will I know the names of the Silly Island players?

Lollipop: I will give you photographs of them so that you know who is who, which is which, where is where, how is how and dishcloth is dishcloth.

Gerald: Do you realise that all the Brazilian footballers will be men?

Lollipop: Really? Well, that's their choice I suppose. It will certainly put them at a disadvantage.

Gerald: Have you arranged for a qualified referee to take charge of the march?

Lollipop: No. Do you think that will be necessary?

Gerald: Oh yes. I have a friend who is a football referee. If I can swear him to secrecy, should I bring him with me?

Lollipop: That's a good idea. I'll give him a copy of the rules, just to make sure he understands what will be happening. Oh, and one more thing – I understand that we might need some spare footballs. Please will you bring some?

Gerald: Oh, Lollipop, I'm so worried for you! Yes, I will bring some footballs. Can I ask you just one more question?

Lollipop: Ask me anything, Mr Tablecloth.

Gerald: Over the past five years I have often wondered how you are managing to generate sufficient electricity. Is the coal mine still open?

Lollipop: Yes, at this momento, but I'm so worried that it might have to close very soon. If we can't find another way to make electricity, we might all have to leave Silly Island. I just can't bring myself to tell everyone. What can I do? Do you have any ideas that might help?

Gerald: I wish I could suggest something, but I'm at a loss to think of any kind of solution, I'm afraid.

Lollipop: Don't be afraid of anything except yellow picture frames. I hope something comes up. It's very serious now. Even the microphone and amplifier for the commentary will have to use electricity being generated by collecting energy from the rotational motion of an exercise bicycle's pedalling system. Poor Mike R O'Phone will be exhausted!

Gerald: Lollipop, I'm looking forward to next week very much. Thank you for asking me to come.

Lollipop: And I'm so happy you can help. Please email me the details of where you would like Woody

Herb to meet you to <u>lollipop@sillyislandcowsill.dot</u> I will make the travel arrangements with Woody. See you soon.

8. What a Show!

Woody and Rosemary were very happy to hear that their daughter had made a new friend. She hadn't had many special friends and her parents hoped she would socialise more. Of course, the McNoodly-Noodly family were very well known across the island and, as Woody said, "They are such a talented family. I'm not at all surprised to hear that Jazz is a drummer as well as being a clever juggler."

Rosemary also wanted to encourage the friendship and told Spring that Jazz would be very welcome to come to their house whenever they wanted to meet. "Thanks, Mum," said Spring, "but I have only met Jazz for a few minutes. We hardly know each other really."

"I thought you mentioned you had arranged to meet him today," added Woody.

"Yes Dad, but that's just for half an hour before the Silly Show. We're just going to practise a short juggling act and then show the audience what we can do. I hope Jazz doesn't want me to do anything too difficult."

"Have you noticed what time it is?" asked Rosemary.

Spring looked at her watch and excitedly replied, "We'd better set off. I'm meeting Jazz in just over twenty minutes."

Members of the audience were already arriving at Sillytown Sillystadium when Spring spotted Jazz, who was wearing a large rucksack, near the entrance to the show. They ran to meet each other, and Jazz excitedly declared, "Look what I've brought." He took off the rucksack and quickly opened it. Inside, there were quite a few items that he hoped Spring would be able to juggle, and they dashed away from the crowds to find a quiet place where they could practise.

A few minutes later, Jazz was delighted to learn that not only could Spring juggle the soft balls but also some of the other things he had brought. Tubes of toothpaste provided an interesting challenge for Spring, but she soon got the hang of how to catch each one without bursting it. They moved on to juggling rolled-up socks, turnips and even coat hooks. Spring was clearly a quick learner, and Jazz happily told her that she was already one of the best he had ever seen.

It was soon time for the show to begin. At precisely 5.12 Lollipop stood in the centre of the stage and opened the show. "Happy Hippetyscringeday, everyone. We have a packed and pickled purple pocket of packets show for you today, so without further delay and diddly-daddlying, it's my pleasure to introduce your friend and mine, Happyjon Umbrella-Zup." There was much applause and many cheers as a tall, gangly youth wandered shyly onto the stage and, after an awkward silence, the sound of bagpipes filled the air. Happyjon's friend Fredfred MacFred played his own composition *The Sound of Froth* as Happyjon, standing on his hands, danced happily for two minutes. Spring, patiently waiting for her turn to perform, sat with Jazz on the front row, trying to remember how to throw the first turnip in the juggling sequence she had learnt.

Jazz helped a rather red-faced Happyjon and Fredfred off the stage to further applause as Lollipop announced the entrance of the invisible crow. "The crow is feeling quite tired today," she announced, "so he or she will perform for just a few moments before we are treated to a surprise finale."

There were many gasps from the audience as people wondered what was in store from their favourite crow. After what Spring later described as 'fifty seconds of nothing', those in the first three rows could hear the distant sound of gargling, lasting for three or four seconds. An old man in the second row leapt to his feet, turned round and shouted, "The crow has gargled!" The response was incredible, with much cheering and cries of, "That was wonderful!", and some of the crow's greatest fans were in floods of tears of joy for the unexpected triumph of their hero.

As the commotion died down, Jazz beckoned to a rather nervous Spring to join him on stage and he personally spoke to the crowd. "Ladies, gentlemen, children and all sillies, I am delighted to present a newcomer to the stage. Spring Herb only started juggling a few days ago and has already proved to be one of the greatest talents many of us will have ever seen. She is joining me today for what I hope will be the first of many millions or even billions of performances. Please give her a big hand." Phil de Bucket appeared from the side of the stage carrying a papier mache model of a huge hand, which he presented to an embarrassed Spring. The audience, still mumbling their approval of the invisible crow's unexpected gargling debut, responded with relative indifference to the appearance of the girl known throughout Silly Island as the granddaughter of the person often referred to as 'THAT man!' However, the first few moments of Spring's juggling alongside Jazz impressed them so much that, once Fredfred MacFred had picked up his new blue and yellow spotted bagpipes offstage and started to play another of his compositions, *Oh Yes, It's Raining Fluff,* to the rhythm of the juggling, people soon started clapping in appreciation of her skills. Balls, turnips, rolled-up socks, bananas and even coat hooks danced above Spring and her face was aglow with delight. As she caught the fifth coat hook for the final time the crowd erupted with cheering and applause, and they spontaneously shouted, "More, more, more, more."

Knowing that they had to present some kind of encore, Jazz whispered to Spring, "I'll juggle the bananas to you, and you juggle them to me. Keep it going until Fredfred stops playing." Spring had no idea how to juggle in this way but, of course, she immediately succeeded as Jazz gave her confidence to express herself. The bagpipe music played faster and faster until it suddenly ended in a cloud of fluff, and the audience all stood, applauding for at least five minutes. A wonderful partnership was born on that Hippetyscringeday.

Further acts followed, as Phil, Phil, Bob, Phil, Phil and Phil the whistling statues and Holly the Human Tree, inspired by the atmosphere generated by Spring and Jazz, performed to intense applause and enthusiastic cheers.

The audience were a little concerned to note that Zenda the Wiggly, who had been expected to perform that evening, was nowhere to be found, but Lollipop returned to the stage to explain that, earlier that day, Zenda had met her friend Glenda the

Giggly, and they were working together on a new act which everyone would see in due course.

"And finally," announced Lollipop, "One of our cowsillors, Hughie Budge, would like to share some wonderful news with us all." She stood back as Hughie nervously began to speak. The islanders suspected that Hughie was about to wrestle himself yet again, and they settled down for a few minutes of strange entertainment. But Hughie was in no mood for wrestling, and he wanted to talk instead, if he could be brave enough to address the huge crowd.

"Football match," stuttered Hughie. "Silly Island and Brazil will play in a few days' time." There was much hilarity among some members of the audience, who thought Hughie must have become a comedian. He continued, by now feeling a little more confident. "If you would like to play in the match, please let me know before you go home." There was something about the increasingly firm tone of Hughie's voice that made people suspect he might actually be serious after all, and a strange silence took the place of the earlier celebratory sounds.

The silence was broken by a lone voice. Four-year-old Herbie Herb, who had been seated on Rosemary's knee throughout the show, shouted, "Can I play?" Everyone turned to look at him.

"Of course you can," answered Hughie, kindly. Other voices followed, as it dawned on people that Hughie was asking for volunteers. Lollipop took control of the situation and said, "It has been decided that the cowsillors should play and, as you have just heard, Hughie has now promised Herbie that he can join the team too. Anyone else who would like to apply to play foot-thingy-whatsit for Silly Island against Brazil may write their name on a piece of paper and put it in Hughie's miner's helmet. I will then ask Herbie Herb to pull out four pieces of paper with the names of players to join Hughie Budge, February April, Leighton Early, Carol Christmas, Jim Nasium, Herbie Herb and myself in the team.

And so it was decided. Hughie's miner's helmet soon filled with pieces of paper bearing the names of those who wished to play in the match, and a delighted Herbie jumped up on the stage to pull out four names at random. Those chosen were Mr Bottle, twig sculptor Eileen Dover, Ed Ache the pharmacist and hairdresser Hermione Q.

As the audience started to make their way home, Jazz and Spring talked about what they had achieved that evening. "You were incredible, Spring," said a happy Jazz. "Can we get together again soon?"

"Thank you for giving me such a great opportunity. I have never felt like that before, and it was good, really exciting. And yeah, let's try some more crazy juggling. Maybe you could drum while I juggle sometimes, too."

"That's a great idea – let's do it!"

82

9. Meeting Dr Cafasso

Dr Alessandra Cafasso marched busily towards the smallest passenger plane on the main runway at Leonardo da Vinci airport in Rome, Italy. With a single-engine propeller and pale blue tips on pink wings, 'The Fly', Silly Island's one and only aircraft, bearing the unmistakeable tartan-patterned *SILLY HAIR* lettering on either side, looked frail in comparison with the enormous jet aircraft surrounding it, but Dr Cafasso knew from past experience that its safety record was second to none and that its pilot was a very special person.

Woody Herb beamed with delight as he held opened the door to welcome Dr Cafasso on board. "It's wonderful to see you again, Dr Cafasso."

"And I feel so happy to see my favourite pilot once more, my dear young Woody."

"Young? Not any longer, I'm afraid. Time catches up with everyone, but you are as sprightly as ever." The two shared a brief hug before it was time for take-off. Woody's flight assistant was Carrie de

Bucket, Phil's daughter, and she helped Dr Cafasso to her seat before explaining flight procedure.

Soon after take-off, Woody turned to Dr Cafasso and, after confirming that Basil was in good health, added, "My father is so excited to see you again. I'm sure you will both have a lot to talk about."

"I have no doubt that's true," replied Dr Cafasso. It will be so good to see Basil again and to spend time with you and your family, too. I have heard so much about you all. The last time I saw Herbie he was still wearing nappies!"

Woody laughed. "Yes, I'm sure you won't forget sharing a few sleepless nights at our home because of his lively activities. He is almost five years old now and his sister is eleven."

"Ah yes. Basil has told me that Spring has extraordinary artistic talents, and I'm so looking forward to seeing what she can create."

"Just meeting you will be such a treat for her, and I'm sure you will encourage and inspire her."

Dr Cafasso smiled and said, "Believe me, the pleasure will be all mine. And now, if you don't mind,

I think I will close my eyes and have a little rest before we arrive at Sillytown Hairport."

A warm welcome greeted 'The Fly' as it landed at Sillytown Hairport, with Basil, Rosemary, Spring and Herbie all there to greet Dr Cafasso. As Rosemary drove them along the narrow main road to their home at Crunch, Spring listened to the grown-ups chatting, which made her feel a little nervous about how Dr Cafasso would react to seeing her paintings. However, concentrating on her other newly recognised talent for juggling and her friendship with Jazz gave her some reassurance that she had nothing to fear when it came to showing others what she could do.

Soon, everyone was seated in Basil's living room and, just as Rosemary and Spring came through from the kitchen with drinks, Herbie decided it was his turn to talk to Dr Cafasso. "Guess what I'm going to do."

Dr Cafasso tried to imagine what a four-year-old boy would want to share with her and smiled, "I guess that you are soon going to be five."

"No... well, yes, but there's something else."

"Oh. Then I guess you are going to sing me a song."

"I know lots of songs but I'm going to do something much better than that."

"I really can't guess. Do you want to tell me?"

"Yes. I'm going to play football."

Dr Cafasso, not aware of the significance of what Herbie was saying, replied, "That's lovely. Football is great fun. You'll really enjoy it. People in Italy love football very much."

Woody decided to expand upon what Herbie meant, and added, "I believe that people in Brazil love football very much too, don't they?" The family laughed amongst themselves, and Basil explained to his friend that Herbie was shortly to play international football for the Silly Island team.

"Nothing that happens on Silly Island surprises me!" joked Dr Cafasso.

Later that evening, after they had all had many friendly and often hilarious chats about life on Silly

Island, Rosemary noticed the time and said, "We should be getting back home now. It's way past Herbie's bedtime."

They were about to leave for their house next door when Dr Cafasso asked, "Would this be a good time for me to talk to Spring about her paintings?"

Spring felt a rush of nervous energy, but this time she recognised it as a more confident feeling. Listening to Dr Cafasso and hearing how she liked to have fun had encouraged her to speak up for herself and she was surprised to hear her own voice saying, "Oh yes, please!" Rosemary and Woody smiled and, after her family had all hugged Dr Cafasso and left to go to their house next door, Spring felt privileged to sit next to the famous artist while her proud grandfather sat in his favourite armchair.

Basil, who had clearly been waiting for this moment to arrive, announced, "My wonderful granddaughter has had a glowing art report from her teacher. I have seen a lot of her work for myself because I saved all the drawings and paintings she has given to me since she was born."

This news came as a complete surprise to Spring, who excitedly asked, "Oh, Grandfather, have you really saved them? Some of them would have been just like scribbles!"

Basil, standing up and heading for the door to his study, beckoned to Spring and Dr Cafasso to follow him. Spring was unsure about just exactly what they were going to find through the door, but what was in there took her breath away. Basil announced, "Look!" and proudly waved his arms around the four walls of his office. There must have been over a hundred of Spring's paintings and drawings there, and they were organised into an order according to her age when she had created them. The first few, from her earliest marks on paper to her first drawing of a person were, to Spring's eleven-year-old eyes, babyish. However, as the progression from age two to eleven showed, the way her painting skills had developed over those few years was astonishing.

After studying the drawings and paintings for a few moments, Dr Cafasso took a deep breath, looked straight into Spring's puzzled eyes and announced, "This is an exhibition of the work of a genius!"

"Yes, yes, yes!" shouted Basil, adding, "and you haven't yet seen her best work. It's on her bedroom ceiling. Spring, please can we show Alessandra in the morning?"

Spring was shocked to hear what the great artist had said about her, and mumbled, "Yes, that's not a problem." Regaining her composure, she asked, "Why do you like my pictures so much?"

Basil and Spring could both see that Dr Cafasso was shaking with excitement, and they all went back to their seats in the living room. Dr Cafasso turned to her friend and muttered, "My dear Basil, you know I hardly ever drink spirits, but…. please can I have a little sip, just for once? I need to compose myself. This is one of the greatest moments of my life!" Basil chuckled, and then brought his friend a small glass containing something he hoped would do the trick.

A few sips later, Dr Cafasso addressed Spring's question. "You ask why I like your pictures so much.

In some ways that is an easy question to answer, but you deserve to hear a detailed reply. I like your pictures very much because they have a unique, highly personal combination of composition, colour and subject matter, and you are able to make those three elements come together to create a unified and well-executed artwork that is a delight to the eye of the viewer. Your flair for composition shows freshness and innovation: that's something that usually comes with maturity as an artist becomes older and more experienced, but you have it right now and we must make sure that no-one knocks it out of you. Your choice of colours is inspired and original, and the spectacular joy within your paintings is formulated by how you apply, arrange, and group shapes in each picture, using those lovely colours. And did you realise, Spring, that you appear in all your paintings? You are so personally and emotionally involved in what you create that I can see you in them all. Do you believe me?"

Feeling quite baffled, Spring didn't know how she was supposed to answer, in fact she didn't understand much of what Dr Cafasso had said, but she could see by the expression on her grandfather's face that she should be pleased, so she simply replied, "Thank you very much."

"My dear girl," continued Dr Cafasso, "what I have just explained is only the beginning. I could answer your question in many more words, delving continually deeper into the reason why great art is great art, but I don't want to confuse you and spoil your own innate response to whatever inspires you, so I think I should say no more tonight other than that I love it all and so will anyone else with eyes that can see. And in the morning, I would be honoured if permitted to see your bedroom ceiling."

"Then I must go home and tidy my room," replied Spring and, after wishing her grandfather and his famous friend good night, she made the short journey home, her mind buzzing with words she could barely comprehend.

The following morning Spring lay on her bed looking up at the faces of her own family that gazed back at her from the artwork on her ceiling. She wondered what Dr Cafasso would have to say about the huge painting, and not only hoped she would like it but that she might use words that Spring could actually understand.

Spring, Herbie and their parents had barely finished their breakfast when Basil and Dr Cafasso arrived. It was obvious to the Herb family that Dr Cafasso was in a highly energetic mood. Declaring, "Good morning. Please may I visit Spring's bedroom now?" she headed for the staircase before the family could reply. Spring tried to keep up with her but was only halfway up the stairs when she heard a cry of, "Magnificent!" and arrived in her own bedroom to find Dr Cafasso lying on her bed and giggling hysterically.

"Do you like my painting?"

"Like it?... like it? My dear Spring, it's your masterpiece! When I look at each family member you have painted it's obvious that you have the skill to breathe life into still figures – that's something I haven't seen since I studied Botticelli's portraits!"

Spring's parents joined them in the bedroom, and Woody suddenly realised that he hadn't even seen the painting before. "Oh Spring, it's lovely," he exclaimed, "but how did you get up there to paint it at all?"

Spring had felt worried that her father would be angry at how she produced the painting but knew that she must tell the truth. "I borrowed your two wooden stepladders from the shed, put a plank of wood across the tops from one to the other and lay on it to paint. I'm sorry, Dad, but you have been very busy recently and I sort of sneaked up and down stairs with your things."

Her father's response reflected his astonishment. "I'm glad you did that," he said, "and I'll help you carry things if you want to paint all the upstairs ceilings." Spring gave her father a big hug, and they all suddenly became aware of a strange sound that seemed to be coming from Dr Cafasso. The gentle "Mmmm" gradually became a louder "Mmmmaaaa" and then erupted into

"Aaaayyesssss!" as Dr Cafasso sat bolt upright on Spring's bed.

"Are you feeling alright?" asked a concerned Basil before realising that his friend was beaming from ear to ear.

"I certainly am, old friend. I have come to the inevitable decision that it is time to introduce Spring to Michelangelo!"

Spring was about to say *'Michael who?'* when she realised that by doing so she might be making a fool of herself.

"It's obvious, isn't it?" went on Dr Cafasso. "The Sistine Chapel ceiling was painted by the great Michelangelo between 1508 and 1512. It is regarded by anyone who has ever seen it as a cornerstone work of High Renaissance art. Our own ceiling painter must see it." She turned to Spring and spoke with a low, almost humble voice as she asked, "My dear girl, please may I take you to Vatican City to see the Sistine Chapel ceiling for yourself? You will learn so much more by looking at it than by listening to me describe its greatness to you."

Spring looked quizzically at her parents who glanced at each other before they responded. Rosemary clearly spoke for them both when she said, "Spring, this is the chance of a lifetime. We would love you to accept the offer."

Without hesitation, Spring replied, "I would love to go. Thank you very much for inviting me, Dr Cafasso." A few moments later, the whole family had been invited to go to Vatican City, and naturally they all accepted. Of course, Woody would be flying them there anyway and Rosemary said that she would ask her colleague, Dr Sammy Samson, to cover her medical appointments for a few days.

Basil was beside himself with joy. Herbie, realising that he had a special day coming too, asked, "But what about my football match?"

"Not a problem," replied Dr Cafasso. "We'll all come to support you when you play for Silly Island, and we'll visit the Sistine Chapel the following day."

"Oh goody-googoo. Dad, can I say three Silly Island cheers for Dr Cafasso?" Without waiting for Woody's reply, Herbie continued, "Hip hip...."

"Hippopotamus," they all shouted.

"Hip hip…"

"Hippopotamus."

"Hip hip..."

"Hippopotamus." Dr Cafasso then saw for herself the traditional six left leg hops, seven right leg hops, two claps and four head nods followed by star jumps and cries of "Eeksie-peeksie."

10. Preparing to Play Brazil

It was the morning of the big match, and the islanders were incredibly excited. Phil de Bucket had worked very hard during the days leading up to the event, ensuring that no-one could have missed the news about what was to take place. The forthcoming match seemed to be the only topic of conversation on the island, and people were to be heard saying such things as, "I don't know what football is, do you?", "Has the Brazil team ever played before?" "How do they decide who wins?" and "I hope Silly Island players know what to do because I haven't a clue."

Hughie seemed to be better organised than usual, and he had arranged for the team members to meet in his garden before lunch. After asking them to sit on his lawn he stood up and addressed them. "Good tootles, everyone. I think we all know each other but I'm just going to ask each of you to stand when I say your name and tell us all a bit about yourself and how much you know about football. I will write down what you say and will put a photograph of you next to your words. That will be passed to Mr Gerald Grainger so that he can recognise you and describe to the crowd what is happening. So, here goes. First, Lollipop, please."

"Lollipop McNoodly-Noodly, leader of Silly Island. I know nothing about foot-thingy-whatsit."

"Thank you, Lollipop. Next, Carol."

"Carol Christmas, just a normal silly person. Football sounds like a silly game so we should all be good at it."

"I agree," said Hughie. Here's Herbie Herb."

"I'm Herbie, I am. Just me. I'm nearly five."

"Do you know anything about football, Herbie?" asked Hughie, to which Herbie blew a very long raspberry. "I see. Next, Jim."

Jim was about to speak when a strange throaty laugh came from a clump of flowers near to where Herbie was sitting. Without warning, the recently discovered tiny hairy creature known as Mister Porridge ran at high speed around Herbie before disappearing across the opposite side of Hughie's lawn, leaving everyone open-mouthed. When the surprise and then huge grins of delight had subsided,

Jim remembered that he had been asked to introduce himself. "Jim Nasium. I'm 88 and I hope football has nothing to do with running because I haven't done any since I was 72."

"Don't worry, Jim," reassured Hughie. "I'm sure you won't need to run unless you want to. Now, Leighton, please."

"I'm Leighton Early. Like Mister Porridge, I love to run and run and run and run so I hope football has something to do with running."

"Next, Mrs February April."

"I'm Mrs April, and I teach at Sillytown School. I hope the Brazilians behave themselves well and have good manners or I will ask them to sit in buckets of ice-cold water and tell us all about what it's like to be a spider in a snowstorm. That should teach them to be good in future!"

"Jolly good, Mrs April. Next, Hermione Q."

"My name is Hermione Q and I'm one of the hairdressers on Silly Island. People sometimes ask me what the "Q" stands for and I tell them it doesn't stand for long and stays sitting down most of the time. I don't know anything about football but who does?"

"Who indeed?" agreed Hughie. Here's Mr Bottle."

"I'm Bottle. I live near the River Water, so I'm Bottle of Water. I think ballfoot would be a better name for the game than football. I'm sure you all agree that it can't be as much fun as juggling." The others nodded their heads in agreement.

"Ed, you are a pharmacist, I believe?" asked Hughie.

"I am. Ed Ache is my name and headache is my game. Football isn't my game."

"Next, Here's Eileen."

"I'm Eileen Dover. I'm probably the only twig sculptor on Silly Island. I can make twigs into most things, but I like making them look like small branches best."

"Aren't small branches the same thing as twigs?" asked February.

"So I'm led to believe," replied Eileen, "but I still think I'm rather good at it. I have tried to make a sculpture of a ball out of twigs but I'm not ready to show it to you just yet."

All the team members were now standing, and Hughie continued, "You all know I'm Hughie Budge because you received my message to come here. I'm the manager of the mine at Dimble, and I must admit that I don't know a lot about football either, but I have written down some rules for you all to read, so I hope they are correct." He held up the ball he had received. "I believe this to be a football. I sat on it this morning, but it didn't squeak, so I don't think it will be much fun to play with."

Lollipop looked into Hughie's eyes and asked, "Do you think we can sit down again now? I have an idea." When everyone was seated she continued, "Look, we don't really have a clue about foot-thingy-whatsit, do we? But I guess that doesn't really matter because the Brazil team must have tried it before or they wouldn't have wanted to come here, would they?"

"A fair point," agreed February, who knew all about fair points.

"So," went on Lollipop. "I suggest that, when the game starts, we all sit down and watch Brazil play for a while and we can join in. By then we'll know what to do."

"A good idea," agreed February, who knew all about good ideas.

"Yes," said Mr Bottle, "and if we still don't know what to do, we can show the Brazilians our juggling instead."

"That sounds like a plan," agreed February, who knew all about plans.

Hermione had a further suggestion. "Just in case our plans don't work, I'm happy to offer the Brazilians haircuts and the latest silly styles. I'm sure they would like that."

"Your hairstyles are the best," agreed February, who knew all about hairstyles.

Hughie felt pleased with how the meeting had gone. Everyone seemed to be reasonably happy with what was going to take place, and he asked them all to meet on Biggety-Big Beach at 2.02. That would give them time to meet the Brazil team before the match, and to chat with them about important things like silly words, having staring contests with cats and standing in barrels for 24 hours.

Meanwhile, the great Brazil football team had enjoyed a good flight from their home country and arrived at a deserted Biggety-Big Beach. They each took a football onto the beach and practised their skills, ready to face whatever their opponents were ready to throw at them. The team manager, coaches, physiotherapist and other members of the national team staff stood together watching the players and looking quizzically at the most unusual football 'pitch' they had ever seen. One other person had joined them on the flight, a tall, well-built man in a dark suit and even darker glasses who stood a few metres away from the rest. He was none other than Benicio Barros, the President of Brazil, and he didn't want anyone to know he was there until the match had finished.

11. The Big Match Commentary

Gerald Grainger, 2.00 pm: Good afternoon, everybody. My name is Gerald Grainger, and I'm here to commentate on today's international football match between Silly Island and Brazil. I'm very pleased to have been invited to your beautiful island by your leader, Lollipop McNoodly-Noodle, who I first interviewed when she was appointed to her post five years ago. I was delighted to finally meet Lollipop a few minutes ago and was pleasantly surprised to hear her say that the Silly Island team are expecting a famous victory over the multiple world champions today. I noticed that the island team contains both men and women, with their ages ranging from four to seventy-eight, and they were puzzled when I explained that the Brazil team consists of men only, with ages ranging from twenty to thirty-two. Hughie Budge, the team's player-manager, feels that Silly Island will have an advantage because of their greater age range, and time will tell if he is correct. You will see that your electrician, Mike R O'Phone, is pedalling to generate electricity for the microphone I am using, and I will stop using it from time to time to give him a well-earned rest.

2.17 pm: With just five minutes to go before kick-off, I'm delighted to see such a big crowd, sitting along the long side of the pitch all the way down the sand dunes. Surely, all Silly Island must be here today. The players have just walked onto the pitch, which of course is one of lovely white sand, and I can see some of the Brazilians straining to carry large stones to where we would normally see goalposts. I cannot refer to the Brazil players by name because they have asked that their identities should not be revealed in order that they may play this match without alerting the world's press to what tactics they might use in the next World Cup. The referee, my friend Mick Symonds, is shaking hands with the two captains. Hughie Budge appears to have won the toss and has asked the Brazilians to take the kick-off. The excitement is building. The Brazilians, wearing their famous yellow shirts and blue shorts, have finished their warm-up and taken their positions, while most of the Silly Island team, wearing a mixture of their favourite clothing and everyday footwear, are standing behind their goalmouth rubbing their heads while patting their stomachs to amuse themselves and the crowd. If my eyes don't deceive me, I believe I can just see Hermione Q, one of the players, setting up some kind of outdoor hairdressing salon within a circle of deck chairs – I hope she realises that the match is about to start.

2.22 pm: Mr Symonds blows his whistle, and the Brazilian number nine passes the ball back to number six. The Silly Island players, except Hermione Q, have now walked over to the centre of the pitch and they are sitting down on the sand. I have never seen tactics like this before. The Brazilians look confused and don't seem to know how to react. Oh dear - number six has passed the ball back towards his own goal but the goalkeeper wasn't looking – he was clearly trying to ask the referee what was going on, and the ball has gone straight past him and into the goal. Silly Island 1 Brazil 0. The crowd aren't cheering, but I assume that's because they have never seen a goal scored before.

2.23 pm: Mr Symonds has asked Hughie Budge to stand up and restart play, and Hughie has kicked the ball from the centre, across the far side of the pitch and straight into the sea. The Brazil number eleven is complaining about having to wade out to bring it back. Mike R O'Phone is beginning to tire, so I'll give him a rest while you enjoy the action.

2.40 pm: Mike is pedalling for all he's worth once again, so I'm back! A few minutes ago I shouted to Lollipop to ask why her team was sitting down and she explained that they were watching Brazil and were going to start playing when they could understand what to do. Since then, the Silly Island team have started jogging or just walking around the pitch, and one of them, Leighton Early, actually managed to kick the ball once. The Brazilians are passing the ball from player to player, carefully keeping possession. It would appear that Mr Bottle is the Silly Island goalkeeper, or it's possible that he just happens to be standing near the goal while Hermione cuts his hair. As I speak, the Brazil number ten crosses the ball into the penalty area, the ball hits a patch of soft sand and it instantly stops moving. The Silly Island player nearest to the ball is young Herbie Herb and he picks up the ball with his hands. The referee has no alternative but to award a penalty kick to Brazil. Mr Symonds shows Herbie a yellow card, which he takes and tries to eat. The Brazil number eight steps forward and takes the penalty just as Mr Bottle looks into Hermione's mirror and happily nods his head after checking his new hairstyle. The penalty taker also happily nods his head as the score is now 1-1.

2.52 pm: Sorry for the delay in my commentary. Mike had spotted the mobile hairdressing salon and remembered that he needed a trim, so off he went. He's back now, looking rather dashing with his new cut, so I can continue. You don't need me to tell you that Brazil are now totally dominating the game and have scored a further seven goals since Mike went for his haircut. I can't remember any of the Silly Island players touching the ball during open play, but it is extraordinary that every time Brazil score a goal, a different Silly Islander restarts play by kicking it into the sea. There was a controversial incident when February April's restart kick went very far out from the beach and hit a passing dolphin on the nose. The dolphin seemed happy to take the opportunity to flick the ball from nose to tail many times before returning it with a mighty nose-pass to the Brazil number eleven, who is still complaining to the referee about having to get wet every time he goes to collect the ball when it is kicked into the sea. Mr Symonds has shown him a yellow card which appears to have teeth marks in it for some reason.

3.06 pm: As we approach half time, and with the scoreline now reading Silly Island 1 Brazil 14, I'm beginning to wonder if Hughie Budge might consider a change of tactics. Booting the ball out to sea after every Brazil goal doesn't seem to be a very positive way to approach a football match, to put it mildly. Mr Symonds has put the whistle in his mouth and is about to blow for a fifteen-minute half time interval, so I think I will dash over to Hermione Q's pop-up salon for a quick trim.

3.25 pm: The second half of this exciting contest has just begun, and I'm trying to get used to having green hair. Hermione Q has run onto the pitch and passed her scissors to Jim Nasium, who is understandably very tired after his first half efforts and has decided to try his hand at hairdressing instead. During my last sentence, Brazil have scored their fifteenth goal and Eileen Dover has restarted the game by kicking the ball into the sea yet again.

3.38 pm: A very worrying moment for the Brazilian goalkeeper. He was about to kick the ball out of his hands when all the Silly Island players ran over to him and stood round him in a circle. They all started singing a song that is well-known across the world, 'The Hokey Cokey'. Incredibly, the Brazil team have now joined in too, and we have the hilarious sight of both teams putting their right foot in and shaking it all about! The goalkeeper doesn't appear to be amused and has kicked the ball over the circle of players, dribbled all the way to the other end of the pitch and scored.

3.48 pm: The Brazilians are obviously beginning to understand precisely what Silly Island is all about. A few moments ago, Carol Christmas fell onto the ball and immediately started scooping up sand to bury it. The Silly Island team charged across the sand to where she was and joined in. The ball has now disappeared without trace. Mr Symonds has asked the Brazil manager for a replacement ball. He has passed it to the Brazil captain who has also fallen onto that ball and started burying it. The Brazil players have now all joined him and are burying the second ball. I think I'm going to join them - here I come! Wheeeeeee!

Mike R O'Phone, 3.58 pm: I'm pedalling and speaking to you all at the same time. Gerald Grainger has proved, if proof were needed, that no-one can resist the chance to be silly on Silly Island. I can see hundreds of people on the pitch now. Some of them are helping to bury all the spare footballs, and others are running round in circles, shouting, "I'm a coconut". The referee has booked at least forty-eight people already. Let's be honest, the football match is over and what is happening now is much more fun. I don't really know why I'm bothering with the commentary, so I'm going to join everyone else on the beach and see if I can start a who-can-make-the-longest-scarf-out-of-seaweed contest. I've stopped pedalling now so you soon won't be able to hear what I'm sa……..

12. An Incredible Offer

A huge beach 'barber-queue' took place after the match, with everyone invited and most staying to continue the fun. Although they had enjoyed the match, including the second half silliness, the Herb family and Dr Cafasso left as soon as the totally confused Nick Symonds blew the final whistle, knowing that their flight to Rome would be leaving early the following morning. The Brazilian team had noticed that hairdressing had been taking place during the match and they formed an orderly queue before taking turns to visit Hermione Q for silly hairstyles. Some of them enjoyed having their hair dyed in yellow and blue to match their kit while others chose to have Hermione's special double Mohican style.

During the barber-queue there was a lot of talking and even more singing. Silly Islanders and Brazilians led songs that are popular in their own countries, with the Silly Island favourite, *Ask the Giraffe* being repeated many times:

"Ask the giraffe if you want to know,
Ask the giraffe before you go,
Ask the giraffe if you want to know,
How to jump over a fire engine.

Ask the giraffe if you want to know,
Ask the giraffe before you go,
Ask the giraffe if you want to know,
How to catch a falling snooker table.

Ask the giraffe if you want to know,
Ask the giraffe before you go,
Ask the giraffe if you want to know,
How to be an underwater astronaut."

The captain of Brazil's team was the first to have his hair cut by Hermione and, as soon as he was happy with his yellow and blue double Mohican, he dashed over to Hughie and held out his hand. "Thank you for playing us, my friend."

Smiling broadly, Hughie replied, "It was our pleasure."

"We are sorry to have defeated you by so many goals, but hope you learnt a lot about the beautiful game and will continue to play in the future."

Hughie looked puzzled. "We will play many times, I'm sure, but you are mistaken when you say that your team won. I think you must have forgotten that Silly Island won the game by fifteen goals to one."

The Brazilian captain laughed, "Another of your Silly Island jokes, my friend! That is one of your best. However, I clearly remember that my team scored fifteen goals while yours scored just one."

"I agree," said Hughie, and he held out a copy of the rules of Silly Island football that had been distributed before the match. "Please carefully read rule four, my friend."

Together, the two captains read the words, *Rule 4: the team that scores the least goals will be declared winners of the match.* There was a brief pause before both men roared with laughter and hugged each other and the Brazilian team captain announced, "Then we are all happy winners today!"

The President of Brazil, with his smart dark suit and even darker glasses, had been watching the match from a deck chair positioned quite a way from the others. He hadn't wanted people to recognise him, and just wanted to enjoy watching the football match, but by the time hundreds of people were singing *Ask the Giraffe* as they danced on the beach, he walked slowly over to where Lollipop was sitting with a drink in her hand. Approaching her quietly and cautiously, he spoke to her. "Excuse me, Mrs McNoodly-Noodly, may I speak to you, please?"

Lollipop looked up and smiled before standing up and holding out her hand to someone she didn't recognise – until he removed his dark glasses and she saw the face of a man whose photograph often appeared on world news transmissions. "Mr President! I didn't realise you had come. You are most welcome."

"Thank you, but please call me Benicio. Your country is beautiful, and your people are so happy. It is wonderful to meet you too. I have heard so much about you."

4

"Really? What have you heard?"

"Everything I have heard fills me with pleasure, apart from one thing that makes me very sad."

Lollipop was puzzled. "Please, explain, Benicio."

"May I sit down, please?" Lollipop pulled up a spare deckchair and the President continued: "Five years ago I heard a podcast, where you were interviewed by Gerald Grainger, and you told him that Silly Island would run out of coal in five years. You explained that you were not able to provide electricity for your people by any other means. Those five years have now passed, and today I met Mr Grainger and asked him what he knew about the current state of the problem. I have also seen that Mr O'Phone has had to provide power for the commentary by creating electricity using pedal power. The situation is now desperate, isn't it?"

With her head bowed and tears beginning to form, Lollipop spoke quietly and sadly. "It's true. I have let the people down by allowing silliness to be more important than considering how we can continue to live here." She looked into the President's friendly face and admitted, "I am going to have to face the truth and tell the people that we will soon have to leave Silly Island forever."

The President took a clean white handkerchief out of his pocket and offered it to Lollipop. "Please dry your tears. The reason I am here is to help you and everyone on this island to find new countries where you can start new lives." Lollipop's face showed considerable confusion and puzzlement, and the President continued, "Ever since I heard the podcast, I have tried to find a way to help you, and I'm now in a position to offer something. In the south of my country there is a town where ten thousand people used to live. Some years ago, there was a lot of serious flooding there because a dam holding forty billion cubic litres of water was in danger of bursting. All the people who lived there were asked to live many miles further north until the dam was repaired. When the job had been completed most of them wanted to stay in the new homes we had provided, even though their original town is now completely safe."

"Why are you telling me this?" asked Lollipop.

"Because I want to help you. I heard so much about how wonderful life has been on Silly Island and now I have seen a little of that truth for myself. Mrs McNoodly-Noodly, I am inviting all Silly Islanders to leave here and come to my country for three months. During that period, you may all live in the town I have described. You could call it Rio Silly. We will provide for all your living expenses, including food, lighting and heating, healthcare and your other basic needs. All of that will be paid for by giving you a long-term loan – your people won't have to pay back the loan until fifty years have passed.

The President stopped and smiled. He could see that Lollipop was confused in a way that seemed to him to be sad and happy at the same time. Lollipop had many questions to ask Benicio, but there was one that she knew was so much more important than all the others. "Benicio, I cannot thank you enough for your incredibly kind offer, but... what will happen to us after the three-month period has passed?"

"I have to be honest with you, Lollipop," replied the President. "At the end of the three-month period the town must again be populated by Brazilian citizens. For that reason, I am shortly to meet representatives from all over the world to try to arrange for your people to travel to new homes in other countries after the three months in Rio Silly. In these new homes they can begin new lives as citizens of those countries. I realise that Silly Island will soon have a new leader and I will, of course, invite that person to work with me as we seek new lands where your people can live safely and happily."

Lollipop took a step backwards and sighed. She was feeling muddled and distressed, and she spoke quickly without thinking what she was saying," Oh my giddy goose and spotty socks!" She paused, and continued, "Please excuse my bad language, Benicio. I feel... stunnerated. But I understand what you are saying and I suppose there's no better alternative. I should be feeling positive about what you are offering, but it's just so difficult to imagine what our future will be like without the island and without each other."

"I understand how shocked you must feel, Lollipop, but there might yet be a way you can all return to Silly Island at some point in the future. While you are all living in Brazil there will be a conference for world leaders to discuss climate change, the end of reliance on fossil fuels and the use of new technologies. It is possible that there might even be an agreement to give Silly Island priority in using these technologies to provide energy. Your new leader will be able to put forward your case, and I will certainly give them my support in the hope that, one day in the future, Silly Island will rise again."

Lollipop knew she should be grateful for what Benicio was offering, but the sad fact that the happy and contented people she knew and loved so well would no longer be able to live as one community was too much to bear. She held out her right hand to Benicio, and the two leaders came together to share a firm handshake.

The two leaders then joined in with a passing group of dancing Silly Islanders and Brazilian footballers who were all singing *Ask the Giraffe*. Lollipop's mind was racing, and she knew she was going to have to find a way to explain to everyone that they were going to have to leave Silly Island but that they could have a temporary new life in Brazil that was, in reality, a stepping-stone to massive uncertainty. Trying to put those thoughts to the back of her mind she decided that, right now, she must try to sing, dance, enjoy the barber-queue and be very silly despite her tears!

13. The Sistine Chapel

The events of the previous day had left Hughie Budge in a state of exhilarated exhaustion. Staring trance-like out of his kitchen window, remembering the wonderful atmosphere that surrounded the big match, he was relieved that he didn't have to start work at the coal mine until midday. Surprised to see Lollipop striding purposefully towards his front door, he stood up and stretched. "Goodeth morningeth Lollipopeth", he said, smiling widely as he opened the door.

"Goodeth indeedeth, Hughieth." Lollipop returned Hughie's greeting, but her smile suddenly turned upside-down as she continued, "Hughie, is there something I should know about the mine?"

"Yes," replied Hughie, "It's a big hole in the ground that I work in." Aware that Lollipop didn't seem to be in the mood for silliness, he went on, "What else do you want me to say?"

"Tell me honestly, and tell me now, Hughie – am I correct in saying that there is almost no coal left in the ground?" Despairingly, Hughie flopped down into the nearest chair, realising that he must reveal the indisputable fact that the mine would run out of coal at some point during the coming month. After he had confirmed her worst fears, Lollipop's reaction was simply to sit down alongside Hughie, and she decided to tell him the reason for the President of Brazil's visit. They concluded that the election of a new leader should go ahead as soon as possible, but that all the cowsill members and candidates should be told that the future of the islanders would temporarily be in Brazil. They must also understand that the next leader and cowsill would have an incredibly difficult task as everyone adapted to life in a new country before having to be split up and sent to different parts of the world. Lollipop decided to ask Phil de Bucket to go round the island, shouting out the news that anyone wishing to stand as new leader should come to a cowsill meeting in three days' time. At that meeting, Lollipop would tell those attending about the plan to leave Silly Island and explain that the rest of the islanders wouldn't find out until the day of the election result.

While Lollipop was talking, Hughie remembered something else that the captain of Brazil had told him after the match. "He said that their President had personally asked the Brazilian Football Confederation to request that we play Brazil because he wanted a good reason to come here."

"Wow!" Lollipop gasped. "That means that the President was looking for an excuse to come here for some time. He must have wanted to help our people ever since he heard the podcast five years ago, and he finally found a temporary solution to our problems when the town that will be known as Rio Silly became available."

There was a pause, after which Hughie said, "What a great man!"

Lollipop nodded. "A huge country showing care and commitment to a small island in need – that's just incredible."

Together, they both added, "Fabadoddle-doo!"

Dr Alessandra Cafasso and Spring Herb hurried to the entrance to the Sistine Chapel, with

Rosemary, Herbie and Basil following close behind them. It had been a long and tiring flight from Silly Island to Rome, then travelling by taxis from Leonardo da Vinci airport into Vatican City, but Spring's infectious wave of excitement ensured that they were all keen and ready to see the great masterpiece on the chapel ceiling.

"I wanted to play more football," announced Herbie.

"You will – when we get home," said Woody, kindly, "but first, we are going into this famous building."

Herbie didn't seem impressed. "It doesn't look much good on the outside."

Dr Cafasso laughed. She pretended to agree, knowing that the large building held such a wonderful surprise inside. "Follow me," she beckoned, leading the way. Just outside the entrance, she asked them all to stop for a moment. "Before we go inside, please understand that no talking will be allowed until we come back out again, so try not to sound excited, even though you will be!"

A few seconds later the whole family stood inside the chapel with their heads tilted to the ceiling and their mouths wide open. Spring was overcome by the intense beauty and was happy to silently take in the sheer magnificence of what she was seeing. The adults had thought it would not have been possible for Hughie to remain silent, but even he was so overcome by the experience that he felt as if his voice simply wouldn't work.

After enough time had passed for them to share such a unique and wonderful moment in time, they found themselves outside once again, and they knew there was a lot to be said about what they had shared. At first, they simply smiled at each other, before Herbie suddenly seemed to release lots of words like a river of surging water. "That was just - well – well – so good – so good – yes yes and – it was – better than – better - than – than – than – football – so – woweeeee!"

After much shared laughter, Dr Cafasso started to explain what they had been looking at. "The ceiling was painted by a great artist called Michelangelo in the early 1500s. Michelangelo was actually a famous sculptor, and when Pope Julius II asked him to paint the huge area of the ceiling he found out about the techniques that would be needed in order to produce the great work we have just seen."

"Is it one painting or lots of different ones?" asked Spring.

"It's a series of something called frescoes, which is when an artist uses a wall or, in this case a ceiling, as a canvas. Sand and lime are mixed together and spread onto the ceiling and the colours are added before the mixture has a chance to dry out."

"Michael must have been very tall to reach that ceiling," commented Herbie. "Was he a giant?"

"No," laughed Basil, "he had to build scaffolding up to the top, so he could stand or lie on it to paint."

"A bit like me in the bedroom," added Spring.

"More or less exactly like you," agreed Dr Cafasso, "and, also like you, he had to paint many people. He started by sketching Jesus' twelve disciples and then decided to add 300 more figures and lots of other wonderful things that represent the time before Jesus came to Earth. The whole ceiling has 33 areas that contain characters from before Christ's time. If you look carefully, you might see some that appear in stories you have heard."

"It must have taken Michael a few days," said Herbie.

"It took him four years," replied Dr Cafasso, "four years of standing and lying at the very top of his scaffolding, constantly stretching and straining his neck to reach the ceiling."

"It's the most wonderful thing I have ever seen," whispered Spring, overcome with emotion and struggling to find words to express her appreciation of the masterpiece. "I could stay in the chapel forever."

During the rest of the day, Rosemary and Woody showed Herbie many other magnificent parts of Rome, but Spring went with her grandfather and Dr Cafasso to a building with rooms that were kept as special places for artists to work. Over a few hours,

Dr Cafasso taught Spring a lot about painting. She explained that painting is a way of expressing emotions and the creation of ideas, and showed Spring how to paint with different brush strokes and a variety of lines, how to use shade, how to produce different effects by pressing lightly or with more weight and how to achieve a variety of finishes with watercolour, oils, acrylics, chalk and pencil. Spring experimented with lots of techniques for herself and proved to be a quick learner.

At the end of the session, Spring thanked Dr Cafasso but added, "I could never be such a great painter as Michelangelo."

"Ah, but you must not try to be him. The best advice I can give to you is to be yourself."

Spring learned so much from the great teacher and, of course, just by seeing and appreciating the masterpiece of the chapel ceiling. Back at home on Silly Island she had produced a large painting on her bedroom ceiling, and she now asked Dr Cafasso how she could paint something even bigger. "I will send you many canvasses that can be clipped together and taken apart so that you can move to a large space to paint," promised Dr Cafasso.

Spring's response came as a great surprise. "It is my ambition to create a huge painting that is thirty metres high and thirty metres wide."

"Then I will need to send you many canvasses!"

Spring turned to face Basil. "Grandfather, I have decided that I would like to try to become the leader of Silly Island, but I will need your help. Please will you do something for me?"

"Of course I will," replied Basil, eagerly. "What would you like me to do?"

Spring explained what she wanted to achieve, and Basil told her he was ready to help but that her plan might be impossible to put into practice. "Oh no, Grandfather," she said, confidently, "we will succeed, of that you can be sure!"

Dr Cafasso waved farewell with a gentle and happy smile as 'The Fly' took off for the flight back to Silly Island. On the way home, Herbie sat right at the front with his father, who explained how he flew the plane safely and always on time, and Rosemary used her phone to catch up on her current patients' progress. But Spring and her grandfather sat together at the rear of the plane, excitedly planning something quite secretive but very ambitious and exciting.

14. The Silliest Thing of All?

Spring and Jazz had become best friends. Their shared interest in juggling had brought them together, and they soon discovered they had a lot in common. Spring admired Jazz's drumming and singing, and she considered learning to play an instrument so that she could join him and extend their act into a juggling musical duo. Jazz was flattered that Spring liked his music, and together they worked on extending Jazz's duck-billed platypus song so that it had a new chorus they could both sing while Jazz played a steady drum beat and Spring juggled salt and pepper pots, spoons and virtually anything else she could pick up.

They were practising the song one day in a spare room in Jazz's house when Lollipop's husband Tim-Tom, who had been painting the outside window frames with dark purple and light orange stripes, heard the singing. He thought the words of the chorus were really funny, and he was soon smiling to himself. Within a few seconds the smile had developed into a chuckle, which turned into a giggle, and before he knew what was happening he found himself lying on his back with his legs in the air, laughing hysterically. He just couldn't control himself, and it was only when the music stopped that he was able to stand up again. Tim-Tom took a few deep breaths before dashing into the kitchen, where Lollipop was reading one of her favourite books, *Chocolate Trees of the South Pole*.

"What's wrong?" asked Lollipop. "Have you been crying?

"In a way, yes," replied her husband. "I have laughed until I cried! Come with me, now," and he went quickly upstairs and knocked on the spare room door with Lollipop close behind him, wondering what all the fuss was about.

"Come in, Dad," said Jazz, who had heard his father's unmistakeable heavy footsteps on the stairs.

"Please will you play and sing that song again, right now?"

"Did you likey-like it?"

"You bet! I want your mum to hear it tootly-too."

"Here goes, then." After a drum roll and cymbal crash the drumming moved forward with more intricacy than before, followed very shortly by Spring's juggling in time with Jazz's beat as they sang together:

"Oh, duck-billed platypus, please stay here with us
Here on Silly Island when it's raining orange juice.
You can stay all day, and then sleep in the hay
Alongside Bertie Buffalo and crazy Monty Moose."

Both parents were smiling by the time Jazz reached the end of the first line, and as soon as Spring's voice joined in with the chorus they were chuckling:

"Bootle smootle criggety zong,
Angle tangle tiddle, giggle at your sock drawer."

There was something about the combination of the drumming and juggling that was funny even without the words, but the chorus, sung in strange high-pitched squeaky but loveable voices, caused both listeners to giggle beyond normal levels. The chorus continued:

"Slippers full of seaweed – yuck!
Chingo bingo wengo tanglesplinge.
Don't forget your knobbly knees,
Fully-grown camels often sneeze.
Barter for a starter, Mister Carter,
Cappy-cap-cap, Gloopy-gloop-gleep.
Never mind the sausages, they don't understand,
Baabaa moomoo neighneigh clang,
Old MacDonald sits on a newspaper.
Wheeeeee, Splat,
BAXTER!"

When Lollipop and Tim–Tom heard the line about camels sneezing, their laughter reached volcano-eruption levels. They both lay on the ground with their legs shaking above them as they struggled to regain their composure.

"So, what exactly is turning you two into gibbering heaps of jelly?" Jazz had never seen his parents behave in this way before. Neither he nor

Spring could quite understand what had happened to the grown-ups.

A few minutes passed before Lollipop could speak. Eventually, she took a deep breath and announced, "That was the funniest, silliest, most brilliantly bonkers thing I have ever heard or seen. You should be so proud of yourselves."

"Oh," said Spring, totally nonplussed by this reaction, "Well, yes, I suppose it was quite good in a way."

"No no no," added Tim-Tom. "It is pure sillygeniusindeedy. Please do it again."

And so Jazz and Spring repeated their song with drumming and juggling…. a total of thirty more times. Each time they heard it, Lollipop and Tim-Tom reacted in the same manner. They really wanted to join in with the chorus but were so overwhelmed with laughter and uncontrollable physical weakness that it was only by the time they had heard and seen it twenty-two times that they were able to join in by gasping the word "BAXTER!" at the very end.

Eventually, after taking a much-needed shower, Lollipop told them they should perform their new act at the next Hippetyscringeday Silly Show. Poor Spring and Jazz couldn't accept that other people would react in the same way as the senior McNoodly-Noodly couple, and Jazz suggested that they should test the reactions of others before deciding whether or not to perform for an audience.

"I agree," said Spring, "and I know who else we could perform to. My family are the most serious people on Silly Island, everyone knows that. My dad will be coming to take me home soon. Mrs McNoodly-Noodly, please could I ask him to come in to see and listen to our act?"

Lollipop didn't hesitate to agree. "Yes, but not only your dad – please tell them I'm inviting the whole family to come in right now."

Twenty minutes later, Rosemary, Woody, Herbie and Basil received a warm welcome from their hosts, and they were all ushered upstairs to the spare room. This time, Tim-Tom and Lollipop stayed outside the room because they wanted Spring's family to respond in their own way rather than being influenced by others who knew the act very well by now.

The Herb family stood in front of a wardrobe, wondering what was about to happen. They didn't have long to wait: there was a drum roll, a cymbal crash and the fun began.

"Oh, duck-billed platypus, please stay here with us
Here on Silly Island when it's raining orange juice.
You can stay all day, and then sleep in the hay
Alongside Bertie Buffalo and crazy Monty Moose.
Bootle smootle criggety zong,
Angle tangle tiddle, giggle at your sock drawer.
Slippers full of seaweed – yuck!
Chingo bingo wengo tanglesplinge.
Don't forget your knobbly knees,
Fully-grown camels often sneeze.
Barter for a starter, Mister Carter,
Cappy-cap-cap, Gloopy-gloop-gleep.
Never mind the sausages, they don't understand,
Baabaa moomoo neighneigh clang,
Old MacDonald sits on a newspaper.

Wheeeeee, Splat,
BAXTER!"

Spring was, of course, correct when she said that her family were the most serious people on Silly Island, and she fully expected them to remain poker-faced during the performance. She could not have been more wrong. At precisely the same moments of the song where Lollipop and Tim-Tom had reacted, all four members of the family smiled, then chuckled, then giggled and finally burst into uncontrollable laughter, lying on their backs with legs up in the air. The greatest surprise of all was probably that Grandfather Basil reacted with exactly the same behaviour as young Herbie, after which he gleefully stated, "I feel young again!"

When they had all recovered to some extent, further repeats of the performance were demanded. Cries of "BAXTER!" were probably loud enough to be heard in some other parts of the island!

Tim-Tom then suggested that all members of the audience go downstairs for refreshments. Spring and Jazz, left in the spare room while they tidied up their equipment, finally had a few moments to themselves. For a while they just stared into space, seemingly in a state of shock. Then Spring spoke: "Jazz, I need to tell you something that I don't want anyone else to hear."

"Is it about Hippetyscringeday? If so, let's talk about it another day – I'm as whacked as a whacked whacker!"

"No. It's about me. I have decided to stand for election to be the leader of Silly Island."

Jazz's reaction pleasantly surprised Spring. "Great," he affirmed, "You would be a brilliantipuss leader, I'm sure."

"And Jazz, will you help me, please?"

"Of course I will. What would you like me to do?"

"Quite a lot of things really. The first thing is to help me to carry lots of stuff. It'll be hard work and will take three weeks – sorry."

"It sounds interesting. Don't worry – I won't let you down."

On that day the McNoodly-Noodly and Herb families became friends for life.

15. Planning Ahead

As usual, Dr Cafasso was true to her word. She phoned Basil and asked him to let the manager of Sillytown Hairport know that Spring's canvases would soon be arriving. "It is so generous of you to agree to pay the costs of a huge military transport aircraft," said Dr Cafasso. "Without your help, we couldn't have found a way to send them all."

"I'm glad to be able to help," replied Basil. "I just hope that Spring uses the canvases well. She's planning something – I don't really know much about it but she and her friend Jazz seem to be plotting."

Indeed, Spring had shared with Jazz the secret of what she was planning. When she heard that the canvases had arrived at the hairport she realised that she was going to have to tell Basil what they were up to, and they both called at her grandfather's house to ask him for another favour.

Basil was delighted to welcome them into his home. "It's good to see you both, but if you have come to perform your singing, drumming and juggling act for me again, I think I should warn you that I haven't fully recovered from the first time I saw and heard it!"

"Glad you liked it," smiled Spring.

"Liked it? Liked it? My dear Spring, I liked it more than anything else I have ever experienced, and it has made me appreciate just how special it is to live on Silly Island, even if the people think I'm useless."

"People think no such thing," declared Jazz, kindly, "in fact they appreciate that your wind and wave turbines were a good idea and hope you understand that you must not feel bad about it. You are the only one who has really tried to solve our energy crisis. No-one else has come up with a solution, have they?"

Basil raised his eyebrows and a smile appeared on his face, "Thank you for saying that. You have made me feel appreciated."

Spring put her arm round Basil's waist and told him how grateful she was to have his help and support, "Grandfather, thank you for helping me by paying all that money to bring my canvases to Silly Island. I'm really looking forward to painting on them. But before I can do that, they need to be moved by road from the hairport to another part of the island, and I think it would cost a lot to move them all."

"I have already thought of that," revealed Basil. "There is a business with lots of delivery lorries in Sillytown. It's owned by a lorry driver called Larry Driver. Should I phone him and ask him to bring the canvases here?"

"Not exactly, Grandfather. I won't be painting here. I need them to be taken somewhere else."

Spring and Jazz then told Basil about the next part of their secret scheme and asked him to promise not to tell anyone about it. Basil listened, and his smile became wider and wider as he heard the details of the plan. "That's just brilliant – no, it's... beyond brilliant," and he immediately phoned Larry Driver.

At the end of the day, Larry's convoy of lorries were on their way to deliver the canvases to the agreed destination, where Spring and Jazz were waiting to greet them and to soon put their plan into action.

Phil de Bucket set off on his latest bicycle trip around the island, grasping a piece of paper on which was written Lollipop's message to all islanders. It usually took him two days to get to all parts of the island and shout out whatever announcements needed to be heard. He loved his work and hoped that the next leader would want him to carry on with it for at least another five years. He approached his first stopping point, the town centre square in Sillytown, where he whistled his loudest piercing note and waited a few moments for the crowds to gather. Then, jumping off his bicycle with the half somersault of a trained gymnast (which he wasn't) he shouted in his loudest and clearest voice, "Ladies, gentlemen, children, squirrels, guinea pigs, baby monsters and all others with ears, here is the news of the day." Phil took a piece of paper out of his pocket and read, "Six apples, four packets of crisps, a bottle of grape juice, two cabbages…"

A voice in the crowd called out, "You've done it again, Phil - that's your shopping list!" There was much giggling from the children at the front of the crowd.

Phil, clearly embarrassed by his mistake, found another piece of paper and continued, "Mrs Lollipop McNoodly-Noodly will soon cease to be leader of Silly Island. You are all invited to apply to be the next leader of Silly Island. Those who wish to do so must attend a meeting, along with the present cowsill members, in Hughie Budge's garden on Friday at 8.18 in the evening."

Another voice called, "What if it's raining on Friday?"

"Then you will get wet," replied Phil.

"What if it's not raining?"

"Then you won't get wet."

"What if someone has hiccups?"

"Does that really matter?"

"Of course it matters. Hiccups are infectious. If everyone in Hughie's garden starts hiccupping, think what it could lead to. Everyone on Silly Island might catch hiccups."

"So what?"

"So what? So what? Don't you remember what happened when there was a yawning epidemic last autumn?"

"No." Phil hadn't finished his announcement and was concerned that people were getting restless. "May I continue, please?"

"Oh, go on then, but don't blame me if we have a hiccups epidemic on our hands."

"Don't worry, my friend, I won't," and Phil gave a little hiccup himself.

Everyone burst out laughing except for the person who had been shouting about hiccupping, who ran away shouting, "Run for your lives, the epidemic has started!"

Phil held up his hands and asked for calm. He couldn't have been expected to notice that the tiny, brown-haired creature known as Mister Porridge was about to add to the chaos by running up his clothing and sitting on his right shoulder for a few seconds. As soon as Phil realised the little creature was there, he hiccupped again, causing Mister Porridge to laugh loudly, before jumping from his shoulder and running at amazing speed away from the crowd. The rare sight of Mister Porridge seemed to settle the excited crowd once again, and Phil regained his composure.

"Ahem! The election of the new leader of Silly Island will take place on Friday 8th September, also at 8.18 in the evening, at Friendly Shirt. It is important that all islanders attend the election meeting because Mrs McNoodly-Noodly will be explaining all about the future of Silly Island."

There was a general murmur of confused voices, and one was heard above the others, "The future of Silly Island? What does that mean?"

Others joined in with such concerns as, "Will there be no more fruit jelly?" "Do we all have to paint our faces orange?" "Have Mondays been abolished again?" "Is there a rhubarb shortage?" "Surely we'll still be allowed to sit in puddles," and "Has someone discovered a cure for shiddle?"

Phil had had enough of this undeserved barracking, and he shouted above the crowd, "Listen, listen, please. I don't know what Mrs McNoodly-

Noodly is going to say, so please be at the meeting and you'll find out for yourselves. Goodbye and happy drobbles to you all." With that, Phil got back onto his bike and set off for his next stop, the small village of Tinyville, with a population of eight, where he felt certain there would not be a disturbance such as the one he had just faced.

16. Lots to be Done

Word about the election spread very quickly, and Phil de Bucket found that most islanders knew about it before he arrived at their locations to make his announcement. The main reason why this particular news was being passed on from person to person was because Phil had said that Lollipop would be telling everyone "all about the future of Silly Island", and there was a lot of concern about what this might mean.

Eva Lution, a sales assistant at *Crunchy Shoes*, which was (of course) a shoe shop close to Basil's house in Crunch, had told some customers that she was tired after a hard day at work, and she used the words, "It's a pity they can't get a robot to do this job for me." One of the customers thought she was implying that Lollipop was going to announce that robots would be running the island instead of people, and gossip soon spread.

Some of the more bizarre tales going round were that the Silly Island football team of the future would all be robots, that a robotic juggling teacher was replacing Mr Bottle, and even that Phil, Phil, Bob, Phil, Phil and Phil the whistling statues had been robots ever since they first appeared on stage - "no humans could be so well co-ordinated as them: they must be programmed machines!"

There was also much speculation about who might stand as leader in the forthcoming election. Very few even considered it: Lollipop was a hard act to follow because she had been so dedicated and hard-working, and a lot of people had already decided that "if robots are going to be in charge anyway, what's the point?" Phil de Bucket had thought about putting his name forward, but his experience of heckling in Sillytown had put him off and, in any case, he wanted to keep hold of the job he already had.

Another person who had considered standing as a candidate was Jemima Mimer, a party organiser who had devised such popular games as *Pass the Feather* (in which a feather is passed around a circle until the music stops, when the one holding the feather has to use it to try to fly), *Make a Chair*

Disappear (although no-one has ever won this game) and *High-speed Slow Bicycle Races* (which has quite confusing rules). Jemima had told some of her friends that she was hoping to be elected as leader, but she eventually changed her mind when she discovered that clouds were not really gigantic flying sheep, and she had to admit to having a misunderstanding of basic science.

Meanwhile, Spring Herb was busily preparing for her own attempt to become leader. She knew her chances of success were low. As granddaughter of the person who had been unsuccessful in attempting to solve the island's energy problems, and as a child well known for being sensible rather than silly, she thought it was unlikely that she would be elected. However, her family showed great confidence in her ability, Dr Cafasso had inspired her and Jazz was showing a lot of dedication in supporting her in her bid to succeed his mother.

Spring and Jazz now spent all their free time together. Basil, who of course knew the importance of their plans, regularly drove them to each other's homes and also to the site where Spring spent hours and hours painting and Jazz spent hours and hours carrying things in support of what she was doing. Whenever they needed a break from this time-consuming and exhausting routine, Basil took them to Jazz's home, where they painstakingly practised their singing, drumming and juggling act until it reached a high standard close to perfection.

With one day to go before the meeting of the cowsill and those wishing to be newly elected leader, Lollipop was preparing too. The realisation that she would soon have to tell others that they were going to have to leave Silly Island was giving her headaches. Knowing that she would have to face many questions from the islanders, she decided to speak to the President of Brazil once again to clarify what would take place on the day of the evacuation. The President had given Lollipop the number of his presidential hotline and she picked up her phone with nervously shaking hands.

President Barros was his usual cheery self. "It's lovely to hear from you, Lollipop. Have you told your people about our solution to your problem?" Lollipop confessed that she had not yet faced that moment, but that she would soon be breaking the news to the cowsill members and those standing for election, so she needed to know more details about the move to Brazil.

"Don't worry – we will do whatever we can to make it all run as smoothly as possible," said the President. "Of course, it's up to you to decide when the people will need to start collecting all their belongings together, but if you give them plenty of time I'm sure they will understand."

"But we don't know how much time we have before there is virtually no electricity at all on Silly Island," explained Lollipop.

"Then you should tell people as soon as possible."

"That's why I will be making the announcement at the meeting to elect a new leader. I hope there will then be a few days of energy left before we must leave. Speaking of which, this might sound like a silly question, but how are we all going to get to Brazil?"

"You can leave that to me," stressed the President. "The planning for your evacuation and transportation to Rio Silly has already taken place. We are sending four luxury cruisers and some of our finest passenger planes for your people. They will travel to Brazil in luxury, and will then be taken from the port to Rio Silly in express trains. As for providing appropriate housing for each family, we will allocate houses after everyone has had a chance to spend a few nights in a hotel. Once they have moved into the houses we will leave it up to your new leader and cowsill to fully take over the organisation of Rio Silly, and to run your new home just like Silly Island for the three months they will spend there."

"I cannot thank you enough, Benicio. Your kindness is beyond anything I could ever have imagined."

With growing reassurance that a lot of organisation had been sensitively put into place, Lollipop felt she could face the coming days with rather more certainty. However, Rio Silly would never be Silly Island, and there would be many problems to face in the near future. She also worried that, when they heard the shock news, those standing for leadership might decide to withdraw.

17. Facing the Facts

The cowsill members gathered in Hughie's garden for the special meeting, looking forward to finding out who would like to be a leadership candidate, and also wondering what Lollipop wanted to announce about the island's future. The Splop for the special meeting was short and to the point:

SILLY ISLAND COWSILL MEETING 34th August
SPLOP

1 Jelly tasting
2 Meeting candidates
3 Organisation of interviews and Sillylympics (Leighton)
4 Confidential (Lollipop)
5 Refreshments

Each of the cowsill members had brought a new item to taste with a spoonful of sugar-free fruit jelly, including buttercup (brought by Lollipop), potato (Hughie), clover and vinegar (Leighton), sweetcorn (February), Brussels sprouts (Jim) and Christmas pudding (Carol). The tasting took place during the arrival of those who wished to stand for the position of leader, and each was welcomed with the opportunity to try a new mixture.

Of course, whenever Hughie's squeaky garden gate opened, all faces turned to see who was arriving. The first was Happyjon Umbrella-Zup, well known to everyone for his incredible upside-down dancing at Silly Shows. "Welcome, Happyjon," said Lollipop warmly. "Would you like to try a spoonful of our Brussels sprouts in jelly?"

"Oh yes, it sounds lovely," replied Happyjon, although he really thought it sounded perfectly dreadful.

Happyjon had just taken his first sputtering taste of Brussels sprouts and jelly when a member of the famous Silly Island football team arrived. "Hello, Hermione," said Hughie. "Please feel free to come into my garden and try this delicious sweetcorn and jelly."

"Thank you, Hughie. It smells like the most gorgeous hairspray," chirped Hermione Q, who of course had a lot of experience of such things. "Mr

Ache is on his way here too - I saw him locking up his pharmacy and he said he would be setting off soon."

Sure enough, Ed Ache arrived a few moments later, still wearing his pharmacist's white smock. Leighton offered him a sample of clover and vinegar with fruit jelly, but Ed decided not to accept, saying, "I'm not sure if there is an antidote for clover and vinegar poisoning, so I will say no thank you, just in case".

Everyone was getting on well, enjoying the tasting (or not, in some instances) and remembering the great football match they had all witnessed. When it seemed as if no-one else would be coming, Lollipop called the meeting to order, and each person sat on the lawn, waiting for her to speak. As Lollipop was about to open her mouth there was another squeak of the garden gate and there stood a rather paint-spattered Spring Herb. The reaction of many was one of surprise - no-one had expected a member of the famously serious Herb family to want to be leader of Silly Island. However, Spring was well received, and she muttered, "Sorry I'm late, I've been…er… busy."

"Ah, Spring, good to see you," said a pleasantly surprised Lollipop as she welcomed her son's new best friend. "I am pleased to see that we have four candidates for the position of leader of Silly Island for the next five years. Our friends Happyjon Umbrella-Zup, Hermione Q, Ed Ache and Spring Herb will be interviewed at my home by myself tomorrow, starting at 8.08 in the morning, and February April will make notes about what they say. On the following day all the candidates will meet Leighton Early on the beach at Beachy Bay at 8.08 am, and they will be asked to take part in five simple tasks known as the Sillylympics. Leighton will write down the results of the tasks and he will pass them to February, who will add them to the notes she will have made at the interviews. Those notes will be copied and distributed to everyone on Silly Island so that people can begin to decide who to vote for. What funsquish!"

"It's a bit disappointingle that only four people are taking part in the election," murmured Hughie, "After all, there were six of us five years ago."

"I agree," said Carol, "but I suppose all this worry about being taken over by robots has put a lot of people off. Who wants to be told what to do by a walking coffee machine?"

Lollipop, sensing that the gossip about robots had spread rapidly, was quick to respond to Carol's theory. "It's not true, Carol. There are no robots on Silly Island and you have nothing to worry about. But there is something I need to tell you all, and it's going to be difficult for you to come to terms with what I have to say." There was an immediate silence, and Lollipop knew the time had come when she would have to tell them the unpleasant reality that everyone would have to face. "What I am about to tell you must be treated as a matter of absolute secrecy. No-one must speak about it outside this meeting. Please indicate that you promise to keep this information as top secret by putting your right hand on your heart and repeating a sentence." There was a pause while they all lifted their right hands to the centre of their chests. "Repeat after me," said Lollipop, "I promise not to tell anyone else this top-secret information."

They all repeated, "I promise not to tell anyone else this top-secret information." A cold, clammy feeling of fear filled the air as everyone listened to Lollipop's description of the problem. She told them it had been predicted that the island would eventually run out of coal and that Hughie, as mining manager, had previously confirmed that it would happen one day, but he has now warned that there is virtually no coal left, meaning that there will soon be no electricity anywhere on the island. With trembling lips and a shaking voice, Lollipop went on to explain that everyone would have to leave the island in a few days' time.

Lollipop paused and burst into tears, as did everyone else. After gasps of horror and a few minutes when everyone cried into their own cupped hands, they started to hug each other, lost in their individual and collective thoughts and fears. This really was the worst possible news, and the garden had become a desperate, despairing place.

Lollipop had to find a way to move on, and she shook herself back into her leadership mode. "Please listen," she pleaded in a voice that somehow sounded very unlike her own. "There is some better news." Again, people started to compose themselves and they all lifted their heads. "The wonderful President of Brazil has come to our rescue. We will all be able to restart our lives in a part of Brazil called Rio Silly for three months. At the end of that time we will have to go somewhere else in the world, and our people will have to be split up and sent to live in many different countries. The new leader of Silly Island will be able to meet the leaders of other countries and they will be able to explain how important it is for our people to be properly cared for."

Lollipop went on to explain that the new leader would also be able to ask the other leaders to consider choosing Silly Island for development by climate change technology, which might eventually lead to it becoming a home once again. Finally, she told the four candidates that, if any of them now wanted to withdraw their intention to stand as leader, they could simply let her know before the start of the interviews.

There was a long period of silence as the reality of the situation became embedded in all their minds. Carol was next to speak. "Why can't we tell everyone else? Surely, they need to know now."

"We will elect our new leader very soon," explained Lollipop, "and, at the meeting, I will tell everyone what is going to happen, and why. It's important that people understand that their lives will change, but that we can adapt to the situation with strong, elected leadership supported by a dedicated cowsill. At tomorrow's interviews we will ask you all about your ideas for being leader while we live at Rio Silly. It is important to keep everyone happy and silly while we can. It's not really possible to say what you will need to do after that, but you will do the best you can, I'm sure."

Hughie decided it was a good idea to bring some cheer back into the rather subdued atmosphere, and he asked, "Anyone for refreshments?" which met with general approval. The meeting ended in the traditional way, before each person except Spring made their way home, miserable and confused but at the same time strangely excited.

And as for Spring, she went back to her work, which she now realised was more urgent and important than ever.

18. The Interviews

Interview 1: Happyjon Umbrella-Zup

Lollipop McNoodly-Noodly: Good of the morning to you, Happyjon. Please take a seat.

Happyjon Umbrella-Zup: And to your good self, Pop of the Lolly, and also to you, Mrs April - It's been a long time since I was in your class at school, but I will always remember the time you tried to teach me to dance. I must have been a difficult child then.

February April: Oh yes, I remember it well. I think that must have been when you first discovered it was easier for you to dance upside-down than on your feet. Oh well, whatever makes you happy.

Lollipop: I suppose we should get down to business, Happyjon. I'll ask you a few questions and February will make notes based on what you say.

Happyjon: Rightio and leftio.

Lollipop: Why would you like to be the leader of Silly Island and Rio Silly?

Happyjon: I want to show people that my life isn't all about upside-down dancing. I believe that I can show people a new kind of silliness that they will love.

Lollipop: Can you tell me some examples of your new kind of silliness, Happyjon?

Happyjon: I have four ideas. Firstly, to make funny noises instead of using words all the time, such as squeaking like a mouse when you mean 'sorry', whistling a very high note for 'goodbye' and blowing a raspberry when you want to ask for extra broccoli. My next idea is to shout loudly in the library instead of being quiet all the time, but only on Hippetyscringedays. Thirdly, to make sure that any untried Brussels sprout mixed with fruit jelly is destroyed, because it's horrible, and anything that's horrible cannot be thought of as silly. My fourth idea is that people should be allowed to change their names every week, just to give everyone something to talk about when they run out of ideas.

Lollipop: Very interesting, Happyjon.

Happyjon: I would encourage people to change their names every week by calling myself Julian Poole in the first week, then Alfie Cupboard in week two, Lenny Lozenge in week three, Daniel Spaniel in week f....

Lollipop: Sorry to interrupt, Happyjon, but I think we've got the idea. I have just one other question. How could you, as leader, help everyone to settle into a new way of life in Rio Silly?

Happyjon: I think it's really important to have a new language for our new country. I would teach everyone a new language that I have invented - it's called *Happylingo*. Just listen to how wonderful it sounds - Gringlo do pinglo do solo morvin grassnostril stickback gringlo yesso boomer chips.

Lollipop: And that means?

Happyjon: It means "hello". Would you like to hear more?

Lollipop: Not right now, Happyjon. I think we've got the idea about speaking *Happylingo*, and it will be interesting to know how other people feel about it. Thank you very much for telling us your ideas.

Happyjon: Jumblo in gumblo bobblo benbinbanbunbonwhirtle. That means "thank you too".

Interview 2: Hermione Q

Lollipop: Hello, Hermione. Please sit down and make yourself comfortable.

Hermione Q: Good morning, and would you like me to give you a shampoo and set while I'm here?

Lollipop: Not today, thankle youze. Another day might be more suitable, don't you think?

Hermione: Yes, you're right, of course. I just can't help myself – when I meet anyone I just want to give them a haircut and style. How about you, Mrs April? Oh, sorry, I almost did it again!

February: Just relax, Hermione, and you'll be able to tell us all about your plans. I will write down whatever you say.

Lollipop: Hermione, please tell me why you would like to be leader of Silly Island and Rio Silly.

Hermione: Do you remember the football match on Biggety-Big Beach? Well, I was shockled that so many people wanted haircuts there, so I want to set up a haircutting salon in that very spot. I can cut hair and make people happy by talking to them about silly things at the same time. I am good at my job and my job is to make people happy by helping them to have hairstyles that are as silly as possible. I want to start a new style that I will call Cue the Q – it will mean bunching up hair on the top of people's heads and styling it in the shape of a washing machine. That should make everyone happy. I could give you a Cue the Q right now if you like, Lollipop.

Lollipop: Not just at the momentarian, if you don't mind. I might try that another day, probably in about ten years' time. I think you might have forgotten something though, Hermione - when we leave Silly Island you won't be able to set up a salon on Biggety-Big Beach because we will be living in Rio Silly for a while.

Hermione: I realise that. What I will do is to take a bucket of sand from my salon on Biggety-Big Beach and tip it out on a suitable place in Rio Silly. I can cut hair right there and we can all pretend we are back on the beach.

Lollipop: I just have one more question, Hermione. How could you, as leader, help everyone to settle into a new way of life in Rio Silly?

Hermione: Talking to people while they have haircuts will be the best way to keep people happy. Those who don't have hair can come to my salon to give me haircuts instead - that way, I can get to talk to everybody. Another way I can help to keep people happy is to tell them bedtime stories. It won't be possible to tell stories to every person every night, but those who are waiting will know the date and time of their appointments, so they will think, "I'm really looking forward to Hermione coming to tell me bedtime stories in only 486 days at seven o'clock in the evening," or whenever their appointment will be.

Lollipop: I see. Your ideas are certainly exceptionally silly. Thank you for sharing them with me.

Hermione: Thank you for whatever I'm thanking you for, Franz-Joseph. Zoomo for now!

Interview 3: Ed Ache

Lollipop: Hello Ed. Good to seeseesee you. Please take a seat.

Ed Ache: Where should I take it? Don't answer that – I'll take it to my pharmacy, so that the customers have somewhere to sit while they're waiting for me to get out of bed.

February: That's very thoughtful of you, Ed. I have always just sat on my thumb while waiting for you, and the chair will be much more comfortable.

Lollipop: I just have a few things to ask youtoodle-oo, Ed. February will write down whatever answers you give. Firstly, please tell me why you would like to be the leader of Silly Island and Rio Silly.

Ed: Well, well, well, the three wells are full of water. To be leader means making changes that need to be made and not making changes that don't need to be made. Not making changes that need to be made would mean poor leadership, and making changes that don't need to be made would mean poor leadership too.

Lollipop: What are the changes that you think need to be made? You don't need to mention the changes that don't need to be made, just for a change.

Ed: The main change that needs to be made is that national 'something' weeks could happen every week. For example, I would introduce a *National*

Furniture Racing Week, a *National Spoon Throwing Week,* a *National Writing in Capital Letters Week,* a *National Jumping over Pencil Sharpeners Week,* a *National Sleep up a Tree Week,* a *National Make a Tower out of Ball Bearings Week,* a *Pretend to be your Next-door Neighbour Week,* a *National Squirting Lamp-posts Week* and, well, many more. Every week would be different. Each national week would be announced at the end of a Silly Show, and they would end at the beginning of the next Silly Show. People could show others what they did during each national week as part of the Silly Show. That is the biggest change that needs to be made, and I would like to be the one who makes it, without making any changes that don't need to be made.

Lollipop: Wow! And how could you, as leader, help everyone to settle into a new way of life in Rio Silly?

Ed: That's an easy one to answer. I would organise a *National Helping-each-other-to-settle-in-Rio-Silly Week,* so everybody would be helping everybody else.

Lollipop: Thank you very muchly, Ed.

Ed: See you later, mashed potata. Now I'll take the chair.

Interview 4: Spring Herb

Lollipop: Come in, Spring. I would ask you to sit on the chair, but it seems to have found a new home. Please feel free to sit on the floor, and I'll do the same.

Spring: If it's all right with you, Mrs McNoodly-Noodly, I would rather not sit down. In fact, I really would prefer not to take part in the interview at all, because I have so much to do, and I can't afford to have even a few minutes away from my task.

Lollipop: To be fair on all four of you, I'm asking you all the same questions, so that February can write down what each of you says. At the election meeting I would like to tell everyone what each of you said in the interview.

Spring: Then I shall give you my answers now, without hearing the questions. Please just tell the people that I said, "Actions speak louder than words." Now, I really must get back to work. Thank you both.

Lollipop: Very well, Spring. You have made your choice.

19. The Sillylympics Begin

"I really don't have time to waste on this Sillylympics thing!" complained Spring when she met Jazz outside her front door early the following morning. By now, she knew Jazz well enough to tell him how she really felt about what she called 'an overemphasis on being silly'. Jazz sometimes had to remind her what Silly Island was all about, but he was beginning to realise that she had a good point. In addition, this didn't feel like a good time to be really silly: becoming leader meant a lot to Spring, and he was committed to helping her to try to achieve her goal.

"The Sillylympics will be fun, though," Jazz told her, "and I'll get on with the long list of jobs you have given me until you get back. Then I'm sure you will have more for me to do."

"I'm so grateful for your help, but I know most of what has to be done is my own contribution. Oh well, I suppose I'd better go and join the other candidates. It's almost 8.00 and my dad is waiting to drive me to Beachy Bay."

Spring started to jog towards Rosemary's car, then turned back to Jazz again and added, "Oh, there's one more thing to add to your list before I go. Please can you contact Mike R O'Phone and ask him if he can make a recording of the election meeting? Tell him it's important for the island's history to keep a record of what happens."

"Leave it to me. Good luck!"

The other candidates were already on the beach when Rosemary's car drew up, and Spring sprinted over to where they were waiting with Sillylympics organiser Leighton Early. Like the other three, Spring wondered why Leighton had a small donkey-shaped bulge in the side of his t-shirt, but no-one liked to mention it.

"Righty-right-the-kettle-of-pumpkins," announced Leighton, "Now that we are all here we'll get started. There are five events in these Sillylympics, not four or six, but five. Not three or seven, but five. Not two or eight, but five. Not one or...."

"Is it alright if we just get on with it, please?" interrupted Spring.

Leighton was quite pleased to stop and collect his thoughts, as he was feeling a little lost with what he was trying to say: "Oh, err, certainly-of-the-day. I'm going to ask you to pin numbers on the backs of each other's shirts so that I don't make any mistakeroos when I write down the results." He opened an envelope and produced four large pieces of card. "Happyjon, your number is 12."

"Thank you," replied Happyjon, "12 is not my favourite number, but it is the favourite number of Edith, my pet wasp, so I'll wear it in honour of her."

Leighton continued, "Hermione, your number is 16, Ed has number 20.4 and Spring's number is 548."

"Great choices for numbers, Leighton," commented Hermione.

As soon as the numbers had been pinned onto the candidates' shirts, Leighton explained what they were being asked to do. "There are five events in the Sillylympics. Firstly, you are going to show how well you can work with other people. Please stand around me in a circle. Each person must be between seven and ten metres away from me." They all stood in those positions, and Leighton continued, "Now, all turn to face me. Who can guess what I have hidden in my t-shirt?"

"It's a donkey," said Ed Ache immediately. Leighton looked disappointed as he removed a very old but very lovely cuddly donkey from under his t-shirt. "Have I won?" asked Ed.

"Of course not," replied Leighton. "Now listen pleasio. I will throw the cuddly donkey to each one of you in turn and you must try to catch it and throw it back to me." Without further delay, he threw the cuddly donkey towards Hermione, but it landed on the sand halfway between the two of them. Hermione stepped forward, returned to her place and threw the cuddly donkey accurately back to Leighton, who clapped his hands together well before it reached him. He rather self-consciously picked up the cuddly donkey and threw it in Spring's direction, but way over her head and out of her reach. Spring turned round, picked up the cuddly donkey and took it back to her place. She threw it carefully back to Leighton, who again clapped his hands far too soon, completely failing to catch it. "I hope you are enjoying this event", he mumbled, more to himself than anyone else, and threw the cuddly donkey for Ed, but his aim was so poor that it flew closer to where Spring was standing. She kindly threw the cuddly donkey accurately to Ed, who caught it and threw it back towards Leighton. However, Leighton had spotted a gull flying over the sand and wasn't looking at the cuddly donkey. It hit him on his chest and, with a cry of, "What's going on, Mummy?" he threw it straight up into the air, high above himself. Understandably believing that it was his turn to try catching the object but spotting that it was about to hit Leighton on the head, Happyjon sprinted forward and nudged him gently backwards to save him from being hit. Happyjon then calmly caught the cuddly donkey and waited to see what would happen next.

Leighton, who had suddenly found himself sitting on the beach, stood up and brushed the sand off his clothes. Ed, Hermione, Spring and Happyjon were all shaking their heads in disbelief. After an awkward pause, Ed asked, "Who won?" and they all tried (quite unsuccessfully) to hide their giggles.

"You all did quite well," said Leighton, nodding at each person in turn, "and you all won." Emptying sand from a pocket in his trousers before taking out a pencil and piece of paper, he announced the results as he wrote, "Number 12, 38 points; number 16, 38 points; number 20.4, 38 points; and number 548, 38 points."

"And how many points for Leighton?" muttered Spring very quietly, so that no-one else could hear.

Regaining his composure, Leighton announced the second event by asking, "Do you all know what a teaspoon is?" They all nodded, wondering if there could be anyone in the world who was unfamiliar with the object. "I have hidden a teaspoon not far from here, and you must find it. Go!" No-one moved for at least a minute, then, realising that Leighton had finished explaining what they had to do, they all started looking around on the surface of the sand.

Using their hands to move the sand around in random places, they revealed very little other than more sand, although Hermione found a half-hidden piece of paper, on which was written *14 kittens are spotted and 6 are green*. She held it up and shouted to Leighton, "Is this it?"

Leighton ambled over to where Hermione stood. He looked at the piece of paper. "Of course not. I would guess this is someone's sillymaths homework. Would you like me to describe a teaspoon for you?"

Hermione smiled a sickly smile and despairingly replied, "Not today, thank you."

Meanwhile, the others had moved to the edge of the sea and decided to enjoy themselves by skimming stones instead of looking further. Leighton called them together - "Time's up. Stop looking and return to me, please." Ed secretly wanted to carry on skimming stones, but reluctantly re-joined Leighton and the others.

"So, the event has ended in a draw. No points for anyone," announced Leighton.

"But where is this mysterious teaspoon?" asked Happyjon, although he didn't really care anymore.

"It's in a drawer in my house," said Leighton.

"But you said it wasn't far from here."

"It's true. The teaspoon is in my kitchen, just beside the toaster. I only live two miles away." The four competitors looked quizzically at each other, and they were all clearly trying to restrain from screaming. "No-one succeeded in finding the teaspoon, so I'm afraid I can only award six points each. I hope you are going to have more success with the next event, which is the one I am most proud to have invented. Are you ready?"

Staring at the sand in despair, everyone responded by quiet grumbling to themselves, wondering whatever could go wrong next.

20. Rabbit, Yoghurt Pots and Escape

While Spring was busily trying to maintain interest in the Sillylympics, Jazz was working harder than ever on the many tasks she had listed for him. He had come to the realisation that she was talented in many ways, and he was in no doubt that she would be a marvellous leader of Silly Island and Rio Silly. However, in the back of his mind was a concern that the rest of the inhabitants of Silly Island wouldn't be able to see beyond her grandfather's failure, and that they might think she was devoid of silly ideas. For those reasons, and because Spring was his friend, Jazz felt responsible for helping her to the best of his ability. During her absence he had to do a lot of lifting, carrying and what felt like making an enormous jigsaw of some sort. He wasn't even sure that he was doing it properly and hoped Spring would return from Beachy Bay before too long.

Jazz remembered to contact Mike R O'Phone, who explained that his friend Patty O'Door was an expert in sound recording. Jazz then phoned Patty, who happily agreed to connect her equipment to her own exercise bicycle pedal system to achieve a high-quality recording. "My little legs will pedal faster than a cheetah chasing a racing car," she promised.

Down on Beachy Bay beach, Leighton had called the four competitors over, and they stood in a line facing him as he explained the rules of Sillylympic event three. "I'm going to tell you a story," he began, "and you must shout out certain words in response to what I say. If anyone does not shout out the correct word at the right time they have to drop out, and the winner will be the person who makes no mistakes. Is that clear?" Four heads nodded slowly, with all of them wondering whatever Leighton could come up with next. "So, when I say the word *you*, you must all shout *rabbit*, when I say *rabbit*, all shout *spaghetti* and if I say *stop* please shout *wobblebiscuit*. We'll start straight away if you are...."

"Rabbit," they all shouted together.

Leighton was puzzled. "Why did you...."

"Rabbit." Again, all four shouted as soon as they heard the key word *you*.

"No, no, not yet," said Leighton, "I haven't started telling the story." Spring was about to ask how they were supposed to know when the story had started, but thought she might be told to drop out if she were to say anything other than the three words Leighton had given them, so she said nothing.

Leighton paused, took a deep breath and started again. "Okay, I'm ready now. Are you rea…."

"Rabbit."

It suddenly dawned on Leighton that the others were saying *rabbit* because they were following his rules, and he must have accidentally said *you*. He nodded. "Ah, I must apologise for the confusion. This time I'll be careful not to say the word that makes everyone say *rabbit*."

"Spaghetti," they all shouted.

Leighton almost jumped out of his skin with shock at the sudden loudly expressed name of his favourite Italian food. He hadn't expected it to be so difficult for him to tell a simple story, and he cleared his throat before starting again. "Once upon a time there was a little rabbit…."

"Spaghetti."

Leighton smiled and nodded. The game seemed to be working properly now. "Her name was Floppety, and she was a very happy rabbit,"

"Spaghetti."

"One day Floppety the rabbit…."

"Spaghetti."

But Leighton hadn't meant to say *Floppety the rabbit* at that point. He had meant to say *One day Floppety set off to the shops.* He made the mistake of trying to explain this to the contestants. "Sorry, I made a mistake by adding the word *rabbit* whe….

"Spaghetti."

"No, I didn't mean you to…."

"Rabbit."

"Why did you all say *rabbit* th…."

"Spaghetti."

"Okay, that's enough of that. Please stop sayi…."

"Wobblebiscuit."

"Why are you al…."

"Rabbit."

"Rabbit?"

"Spaghetti."

"Stop!"

"Wobblebiscuit"

"Please, please, please stop!

"Wobblebiscuit, wobblebiscuit, wobblebiscuit."

Leighton felt as if the whole world was shouting at him and he didn't know why. He yelled, "Please can you all stop?" and he fell to the ground, covering his ears with his hands.

"Rabbit wobblebiscuit!" Hermione, Ed, Spring and Happyjon were all laughing by now, but Leighton simply couldn't bring himself to join in with their mirth. Finally, after a few deep breaths, he stood up and announced, "That's the end of event three, which was a four-way tie, and so you all receive 52 points for being so clever."

"Please can we get straight on to the next event?" asked Spring, who was feeling the pressure caused by what she saw as a ridiculous waste of her valuable time.

Feeling totally confused and with a headache, Leighton felt like abandoning the entire Sillylympics, but decided it would be a good idea to get it over with as soon as possible. "Very well," he agreed. "Event four is going to be such funnity-fun. In my bag I have four empty yoghurt pots, one for each of you. You must find a space on the beach and, using the yoghurt pot only, dig down through the sand until you reach the other side of the world. The first one to reach the other side of the world wins. You have three years to complete the event. Go!"

Ed was about to complain that the event was totally nonsensical, but Hermione was the first to react. "Leighton, with the greatest respect I must object. We all know that we will have to leave Silly Island very soon. Even if it were possible to dig a hole through the entire planet, which it isn't, we simply don't have three years to spare."

Leighton hadn't thought of this, and replied, "I see your point. Very well then, instead of three years you can have three minutes to complete the task. Go!"

Each competitor picked up a yoghurt pot and wandered out across the beach. Looking over his shoulder, Happyjon noticed that the exhausted Leighton was fast asleep on the edge of the sand. Pointing this out to the others, he quietly suggested, "Should we go back to Leighton, wake him up and tell him that while he was asleep, we all dug through to the other side of the world and came back again?"

The other three were all on the verge of agreeing to Happyjon's plan, but Hermione pointed out that no-one on Silly Island must ever tell a lie, so when they thought three minutes had passed, they simply returned to Leighton and waited for him to wake up. Ed then passed on the sad news that none of them had quite managed to dig all the way through the entire world. Rubbing his eyes and yawning, Leighton said, "Ha ha, that's a good joke, Ed. I know you all reached the other side of the world because I saw you there – we were all riding an elephant up a mountain of ice cream……. or was that a dream? Anyway, well done. 88 points to each of you."

"I'm sure you all agree that the Sillylympics has been absolutely wonderful," went on organiser-in-chief Leighton, "but I'm sorry to say that we now come to our final event, which is called *Leaving Silly Island*." The four competitors were all kindly people who would never hurt anyone's feelings, and they gave Leighton a short round of applause and cheery nods of their heads. "As you know," Leighton continued, "we will all be leaving Silly Island soon, but in Sillylympic event five you must show me that you can escape from the island and come back again within the next 24 minutes and 24 seconds. Your time starts now."

Happyjon, Hermione and Ed were motionless for a good thirty seconds, wondering how to leave the island for a very short period only. Spring, on the other hand, walked along the beach, eventually stopping a good 50 metres away from the others. She then closed her eyes and held out her arms in front of her.

A few moments later, Hermione walked towards the spot where a stream flowed into the sea.

She had noticed what remained of a rather thick tree branch that had been deposited at the mouth of the stream, and started to drag it towards the sea.

After running on the spot for a couple of minutes, Happyjon shouted, "Watch me leave the island," and, when he could see that Leighton was looking in his direction, he ran straight into the shallow sea and continued until the water level reached just below his chest. Then, from almost 80 metres away, he called, "Watch me return to the island," and ran all the way back to Leighton.

Meanwhile, Hermione carefully laid one end of her branch into the water, leaving half of it still on the beach. "Leighton, I'm ready," she announced, then climbed up onto the branch and slowly, with her arms out beside her rather like a tightrope walker balancing high above the ground, walked along it until she stood on the part of the branch that lay in the edge of the sea. "I have left the island by walking across my bridge to nowhere," she explained, "and now I'm coming back." Skilfully maintaining her balance, Hermione turned and retraced her slow but sure route back onto the sand and stepped onto Silly Island once more.

Leighton was congratulating Happyjon and Hermione for completing event five when they heard a call of, "Ready!" from the edge of the sand dune that was closest to the beach. It came from Ed and was followed by his loud and clear announcement. "Watch me – I'm about the leave Silly Island for a couple of seconds." He ran along the dune and, when he got to the steep side of it that fell towards the beach, jumped high into the air. "I'm flying!" he screamed, before landing on the soft sand and adding, "I'm back now."

Ed rejoined Hermione and Happyjon, and the three of them shook hands in the knowledge that they had all found a way of leaving Silly Island and returning. Leighton, however, was heading along the beach to where Spring still stood with eyes closed and arms held out in front of her. Something about her motionless grace made Leighton sense that he should speak quietly. "Spring, it's time to finish now."

Spring slowly opened her eyes and put her arms down by her side. She turned her head slowly towards Leighton and murmured, "That was lovely."

It was obvious that Leighton didn't realise what Spring meant and, as the others came over to join them, he said, "I'm sorry you didn't leave the island, Spring."

"Oh, but I did leave the island," she patiently replied. "I closed my eyes and started to think of a wonderful place a long way from Silly Island. It's a chapel called Sistine in Vatican City, and I could feel that I was standing inside it, looking up at the most wonderful paintings I have ever seen. The colours and the forms brought me such happiness, and I'm so grateful that I can experience being there any time I need to. I was there just a few minutes ago, but I'm back with you now."

Ed, Hermione, Happyjon and Leighton looked into Spring's expressive shining eyes and instantly knew she was telling the truth. Her journey to the Sistine Chapel had been real to her, and the others realised that she had experienced something beyond their own simple efforts. Leighton smiled and his verdict showed a rare grasp of a kind of wisdom. "You have all succeeded in completing event five. 99.9 points to each of you."

Together, they all shouted, "Rabbit!"

21. A National Emergency

Seated in his office at the coal mine, Hughie Budge was thinking about the five years he had spent as a member of the Silly Island cowsill. A great deal had been achieved under Lollipop's inspiring leadership, but now, with just one day to go before the meeting to elect a new leader, he had mixed feelings about his own position. Despite the progress made in many aspects of island life, the fact that it was all coming to an end weighed heavily on Hughie's mind. He hadn't been able to be silly for many days, simply because he was feeling guilty that he hadn't told everyone much sooner about the seriousness of the mining situation. Very sadly, Hughie was about to find out that things were much worse than even he could have imagined.

Hughie's assistant manager, Tony Owl, had just made a terrible discovery. Working on the coal face, his coal-extracting drill head made a sudden screeching sound that could mean only one thing. Tony's helmet torch shone directly into the spot from where the sound had originated, and he felt a jolt of despair all the way through his body. He dropped everything and immediately headed out of the mine in the direction of Hughie's office. The rest of the miners were busy loading coal into a waiting truck, so they had no knowledge of the terrible discovery that was taking place so near to them.

As soon as Hughie saw Tony's tear-soaked face he knew what the bad news was going to be. Struggling to catch his breath, Tony came straight to the point, "That's it, boss. I can't believe what's happened to me. I just took out the last bit of coal from the mine. It's done. We're all in trouble."

Hughie felt as if the ground had opened to swallow him up, but he took a deep breath and kindly gave Tony a glass of water. "It's not your fault Tony. You were just doing your job. Thank you for telling me."

"But boss, doesn't that mean that we won't even be able to switch on an electric light from now on?"

"We have a little time left, Tony. The last two trucks full of coal are setting off to the power station this morning."

"Yes boss, but...but...then we're in trouble aren't we? Surely we can't keep this news to ourselves."

Of course, Hughie had promised not to tell anyone that the island would have to be evacuated, and that plans to relocate everyone were already in place. However, he needed Tony to keep the bad news to himself for just one more day, and said, "I can't tell you much about what's going to happen, old friend, but we are going to be fine. You'll hear the full story at the election meeting, so until then, please hold your tongue."

Tony put out his tongue and held the tip between his thumb and index finger, saying, "Mu mu mu", which is how "Okay boss," sounds when speaking while holding your tongue. Hughie stood up, put on his coat and told Tony to stay in the office until he returned from an urgent meeting with Lollipop McNoodly-Noodly. Striding through the yard, Hughie saw the final truck full of coal leaving the mine, and he called to the other miners, "Well done, everyone. Now you can all take the rest of the day off!"

Twenty minutes later Lollipop learned of the awful news. She and Hughie shared the knowledge that Silly Island was now in a state of national emergency, even though the rest of the islanders couldn't be told just yet. After considering whether to inform the rest of the cowsill and the election candidates about the truth of the situation, Lollipop decided that nothing could be gained by immediately upsetting everyone, and that the arrangement for explaining the evacuation to Rio Silly at the election meeting would go ahead as planned. Hughie agreed with this course of action and returned to his office: he would be the first islander to sort out his belongings and begin packing.

When Hughie reached the office, Tony Owl, still physically holding his tongue, asked, "Mu, mu m mmuu, mmuuuu?" Hughie answered this question by gently lifting Tony's right hand away from his face and nodding, simply because he felt too emotionally drained to speak.

Alone again, Lollipop's thoughts were filled with sadness and concern for all the people. She was also fearful of what she had to do. Standing up in front of thousands of people to tell them they must prepare to leave Silly Island forever was going to be a moment of the deepest heartbreak not only for her but for everyone hearing the news. Explaining to them about Brazil and three months in Rio Silly followed by even more uncertainty was going to be incredibly challenging: Lollipop could imagine the response of a huge crowd – they would be victims of a disaster, being forced to do something they could never have imagined, and the brief benefits being provided by the Brazilians would mean very little to them.

After many tears and confused thoughts, poor Lollipop decided that there was just one person who might be able to offer her some support, and she phoned the President of Brazil, who had given her his personal number.

"It's great to hear your voice again," said President Barros. "Are preparations going well?"

"They were, until today," replied Lollipop, going on to explain that only her own cowsill members and the four leadership candidates were aware of the agreement to relocate everyone to Rio Silly. She then told the President that, because there would be no way at all of providing any more electricity on the island in approximately two days' time, the move to Brazil would need to be organised immediately.

The President was his usual positive self. "No problem! Our ships and aircraft are on standby to leave with just an hour's notice and they will arrive at the island precisely when they are needed."

Lollipop was delighted. "That's amazing," she replied. "I cannot thank you enough, Benicio."

"There's one more thing I can do that might be useful. If you feel that you need my support when you speak at the election meeting, I can stand right next to you. I could tell your islanders about Rio Silly and answer the many questions they will have." For a moment, Lollipop was speechless, feeling such deep gratitude to this incredible person. The President broke the silence: "Lollipop, are you still there?"

"I certainly am, and I would love to take you up on your wonderful offer."

"Very good! I will join you in a few hours. Now, stop worrying and relax by doing something silly for a few hours in the way you always have!"

After the call had ended, Lollipop decided that the President's suggestion was a good one, and she picked up her water pistol, filled it with water, then ran outside into her garden and thoroughly soaked all the washing she had hung out to dry just before Hughie had arrived.

22. Imminent Floodlight Failure

At 8.12 pm on the evening of the election meeting, an incredibly nervous Lollipop McNoodly-Noodly took her seat in the centre of the stage at Friendly Shirt. The meeting to elect the next leader of Silly Island was due to begin at 8.18, and Lollipop was not looking forward to telling everyone that it was time to pack their belongings and leave their homeland forever. Seated to the right of Lollipop were her faithful cowsill members, Hughie Budge, Carol Christmas, Leighton Early, February April and Jim Nasium. To her left were five empty chairs, ready and waiting for the four candidates and a special guest.

Phil de Bucket had already warned Lollipop that many of the people had been anxious when he'd said that there would be an announcement about the future of Silly Island, and that all kinds of rumours were spreading - the most commonly heard gossip was that a hiccups epidemic had taken hold, and many of the nervous islanders had asked pharmacist Ed Ache for hiccup cures. (He recommended saying 'fishcakes' to hedgehogs, which he knew to be as useless as any other supposed 'cures' for the harmless condition). As Lollipop gazed out to the floodlit crowd of almost eleven thousand others who all seemed to be staring back at her, she felt like someone who had been tried and found guilty of a horrendous crime.

Eventually, Mike R O'Phone and Patty O'Door started pedalling side by side to produce enough electricity to power Lollipop's microphone and the high-quality recording equipment. Shakily, Lollipop got to her feet and began to speak. "Welcome, everyone, to this election meeting. Before I introduce the candidates, I would like you to join me in a huge 'thank you' to Carol, Leighton, Hughie, Jim and February, who have been the most wonderfulelastic cowsill for the past five years." Immediately, there was thunderous applause and cheering which reflected the satisfaction and gratitude of the entire population of the island, but made Lollipop wonder what a contrast there was going to be when she gave them the bad news in just a few more minutes. She continued - "And now I would like to introduce our special guest. I'm sure you all remember the day Silly Island played a foot-thingy-whatsit match against Brazil." There were many cries of *fifteen-one, fifteen-one, fifteen-one, fifteen-one*, and Lollipop had to hold up her hands to quieten the crowd in order to continue. "On that day we made friends with the Brazilians and had lots of sillipendous fun with them. And one of our new friends has travelled all the way from Brazil to be with us tonight – here he is, President Benicio Barros!" Remembering the fun and singing shared with the Brazilians at the after-match barber-queue, the crowd spontaneously started singing the song that so many had shared on that occasion:

> *"Ask the giraffe if you want to know,*
> *Ask the giraffe before you go,*
> *Ask the giraffe if you want to know,*
> *How to jump over a fire engine.*

> *Ask the giraffe if you want to know,*
> *Ask the giraffe before you go,*
> *Ask the giraffe if you want to know,*
> *How to catch a falling snooker table.*

Ask the giraffe if you want to know,
Ask the giraffe before you go,
Ask the giraffe if you want to know,
How to be an underwater astronaut."

President Barros joined in with the singing as he walked onto the stage and took his place at Lollipop's side. "You're doing well," he whispered to her. "Don't worry about a thing. I'm here now and I'll help you all the way from here to Rio Silly."

Encouraged by his words, Lollipop asked the crowd to look at the printed sheets they had been given as they came into Friendly Shirt that evening. They contained information about the four candidates, including the results of the Sillylympics, which Lollipop described as being, "designed to test the mental, physical and silly attributes of the candidates." She continued, "The final points awarded to each candidate were as follows: Happyjon Umbrella-Zup, 277.9; Hermione Q. 277.9; Ed Ache, 277.9; Spring Herb, 277.9." When it had sunk in that everyone had achieved the same total number of points, the crowd immediately burst out laughing. However, when Lollipop explained that 277.9 was a high score, which showed that the candidates had all shown a high level of silliness, the laughter turned to sincere applause.

Next, Lollipop introduced the four would-be leaders one by one. "Please show your appreciation for the first candidate, Happyjon Umbrella-Zup." Happyjon walked onto the stage, waving to the crowd who all waved back, and sat next to the President of Brazil. "As you can see from your sheet," said Lollipop, Happyjon would like us to sometimes make silly noises instead of words, to shout loudly in the library on Hippetyscringedays, to destroy all Brussels sprouts mixed with fruit jelly recipes and to allow us to change our names every week." Happyjon smiled when he heard a ripple of applause, and then, predictably, he danced upside-down, clapping his feet in the air until the President of Brazil gave him a stern glance that suggested he should sit down again.

"Now I'm pleased to introduce our second candidate, someone who many of you visit whenever you can, our hairdresser Hermione Q." Hermione walked slowly and carefully onto the stage wearing what can best be described as an outrageous wig. Almost as high as herself, Hermione's imitation blue and green horizontally striped hair was in the shape of a space rocket with letters made of sparkly buttons spelling out "SILLY ISLAND TO THE MOON" fixed all the way down the front from top to bottom. The crowd burst out laughing and some of the younger ones repeatedly jumped into the air like rockets taking off. Eventually, Lollipop was able to continue. "Hermione would like to give you lots of new hairstyles, including her own invention *Cue the Q*, which involves bunching up hair on the top of your heads and styling it in the shape of a washing machine. She would also like you to go to sleep happily when she tells you bedtime stories." Hermione stood up to take a bow, but as she did so the top stage of her rocket wig fell into the lap of President Barros, who put it onto his own head, much to the amusement of everyone except Hermione, who flopped sadly down into the chair next to Happyjon Umbrella-Zup.

"Next," continued Lollipop, "let's have a round of applause for Ed Ache, our popular pharmacist." Ed walked on to rapturous applause, mainly because people were grateful for his recent anti-hiccup advice, and took his seat next to Hermione. "If you elect him as leader, Ed will organise special weeks, such as a *National Squirting Lamp-posts Week*, a *National Furniture Racing Week*, a *Jumping over Pencil Sharpeners Week*, a *National Sleep up a Tree Week, a Pretend to be your Next-door Neighbour Week*, and lots of others." In order to encourage voters, Ed held out a surprisingly large pencil sharpener before putting it onto the floor and leaping over it: it would be fair to say that the crowd was underwhelmed by this display.

"And now, the youngest of our candidates, Spring Herb," declared Lollipop. People lifted their hands, ready to clap, but it was soon apparent that Spring was not going to appear in person.

After an awkward pause, Lollipop was as astonished as everyone else when Jazz walked confidently onto the stage, headed for the microphone and announced, "Spring has asked me to read this message to you all," He took a piece of paper out of his pocket and read, "Actions speak louder than words." An eerie silence followed, simply because no-one knew how they should react, and an expressionless Jazz walked slowly from the stage.

Lollipop felt that the strange silence was somehow stopping her vocal cords from working, but she knew that the time had come when she must face her final responsibility as leader. What she was about to say was going to cause a deep upset for the people who had always trusted her. President Barros turned to Lollipop and, gently squeezing her hand, gave her his best reassuring smile. She cleared her throat and began, "As your leader I have always tried to do my best, and you have supported me in all I have done over the past five years. But now I must tell you that I have let you down…." And as Lollipop spoke, the floodlights started to flicker on and off. Some people gasped but continued to listen to their leader's speech with concerned faces. "I have let you down because I didn't act soon enough when..." and at that moment her voice couldn't be heard at all because very loud, fast drumming, coming from the back of the stage suddenly drowned out everything she was trying to say. The members of the cowsill, the candidates, the President of Brazil and an utterly confused Lollipop picked up their chairs and moved quickly to either side of the stage because they had seen a drum kit on some sort of moveable ramp heading towards where they had been sitting. The ramp was being pushed forward by Tim-Tom, Rosemary and Woody, and Jazz had begun to play his drums like never before, using all his physicality and skill to produce the most incredibly brilliant solo anyone had ever heard. The floodlights continued to flicker on and off, and their impending failure helped to create an atmosphere of amazing suspense amidst the excitement of the extraordinary drumming. As the drum kit reached the front of the stage, Herbie Herb celebrated his fifth birthday by leaping up and dancing crazily in front of Jazz's drums.

The crowd were loving it! Cheering and clapping with more and more enthusiasm for this unexpected and brilliant entertainment, they hardly noticed that the floodlights were failing more and more. Lollipop, Hughie and the President knew that the electric lighting couldn't last much longer - the final pieces of coal from the last ever lorryload were being burnt in the power station and the inevitable disaster was about to strike.

23. An End – and a New Beginning

The crowd noticed that someone else had appeared at the front of the stage. Basil Herb stood next to his dancing grandson, and those who had attended his failed attempt at creating wind-powered energy five years earlier noticed that he was carrying the brown suitcase which once again contained his control panel. He opened the suitcase, took out the control panel and, just as he had done once before, pressed a big red button. Part of the ground, just behind the stage, slid slowly open. Strange grinding sounds sensationally mingled with Jazz's wonderful drumming as, for only the second time in the history of Silly Island, the great wind turbine slowly rose up from out of the ground. By this time, the floodlights were half on, half off, with the light deteriorating every minute. However, it was clear and obvious to everyone watching that something was attached to the blades of the turbine.

Over the previous days and weeks, Spring had been working day and night to achieve her ambition of painting an enormous work of art and having it attached to the lower part of the wind turbine. Jazz, with some help from Basil, had clipped together the canvases which Dr Cafasso had provided, and the painting was now complete.

The painting slowly emerged as if from the earth. Being thirty metres high and thirty metres wide, it was breathtaking and unique. The whole painting was revealed as the wind turbine continued to rise and, when it reached its maximum height of 306 metres, the artist finally appeared. Spring ran to the front of the stage and stood next to her grandfather. Now that the work had been revealed in all its glory the islanders finally realised that the subject of the painting was the silliness of the Silly Islanders. Spring had painted many of them doing the silly things they loved best. Details included Mr Bottle juggling rhubarb, Zenda in mid-wiggle, Leighton Early winking at a tree, Hughie Budge wrestling himself, the statuesque Phil, Phil, Bob, Phil, Phil and Phil, Norman Conquest's gurple falling into the pond, the Yllis family wearing hilarious false noses, schoolchildren in flannel-throwing classes,

Fredfred MacFred with his yellow spotted bagpipes, Holly the human tree and even the invisible crow (depicted by an empty crow-shaped space in the top right-hand corner). Many other islanders appeared on the painting, all of them in characteristic silly situations. It was obvious to everyone that the painting was a work of genius - the colours, forms, brushstrokes, contrasts, use of light and shade, patterns and, of course, portraiture were all of the highest possible standard.

Although the floodlights were becoming more and more dim, once the islanders noticed what the painting was portraying, they started to laugh. Some were laughing at themselves, some at others they recognised, but they were all reaching a state of gigglesomeness rarely heard, even on Silly Island.

As the laughing continued to build in intensity Spring and Jazz put the second part of Spring's plan into action. She hurriedly dashed over to Mike R O'Phone and Patty O'Door and virtually begged them to pedal as never before, adding, "The future of Silly Island depends on you." She immediately ran back to the centre of the stage and shouted "Now!" to Jazz. After a pause in the drumming that represented the beginning of the next phase, Jazz played his much-practised drum roll and cymbal crash, and Spring immediately began to juggle her selection of many objects. The crowd, already excited by the painting and on the verge of yet more laughter, finally got to hear and see what Spring and Jazz had been preparing. The words of their song were amplified more than ever, thanks to Mike and Patty's phenomenal pedalling:

"Oh, duck-billed platypus, please stay here with us
Here on Silly Island when it's raining orange juice.
You can stay all day, and then sleep in the hay
Alongside Bertie Buffalo and crazy Monty Moose.

Bootle smootle criggety zong,
Angle tangle tiddle, giggle at your sock drawer.
Slippers full of seaweed – yuck!
Chingo bingo wengo tanglesplinge.
Don't forget your knobbly knees,
Fully-grown camels often sneeze.

Barter for a starter, Mister Carter,
Cappy-cap-cap, Gloopy-gloop-gleep.
Never mind the sausages, they don't understand,
Baabaa moomoo neighneigh clang,
Old MacDonald sits on a newspaper.
Wheeeeee, Splat,
BAXTER!"

Spring and Jazz were not at all surprised that the level of laughter grew as the song progressed. The chuckling increased throughout the first four lines, and by the time the chorus reached *"Angle tangle tiddle, giggle at your sock drawer"*, sung in Spring and Jazz's strange high-pitched but loveable voices, some people had already reached uncontrollable levels of laughter. When they heard the line about camels sneezing, reactions were beyond extreme. Very soon, every member of the crowd lay on the ground with their legs shaking above them, struggling to regain their composure.

Encouraged by this incredible reaction, Spring's juggling became more and more exciting to behold. As the song was repeated, with both performers singing loudly and clearly, she tossed different objects to different heights, with tennis balls sailing above head height, then skittles a little higher still, followed by the wildly spinning bananas and finally the almost unbelievable sight of sticks of rhubarb reaching into the dark sky above the stage. As each item fell back towards her, Spring caught them and immediately released them again before spinning round and round in a dizzying display that was more like a speeded-up film than reality. Many members of the crowd were jumping up and down in time to the flying objects, but others found that the silliness-induced weakness in their legs seemed to paralyse them.

The chorus was repeated over again, with Spring adding more and more juggling techniques each time, and the crowd continuing their extreme helplessly silly behaviour while joining in with each cry of "BAXTER!" But suddenly, after six repeats of the chorus, the floodlights flickered for the last time, and they stopped working altogether. Friendly Shirt was plunged into total darkness and a sudden eerie silence. Spring was unable to see what she was juggling and, no longer able to catch, she fell to her knees. Five seconds passed, then ten, and no sound could be heard. It was as if no-one was there at all.

Then a voice broke through the silence and darkness. Basil was calling to his granddaughter. "Now, Spring, now. Remember, actions speak louder than words! Talk to your people."

Hearing this distant voice, Mike and Patty nudged each other and started to pedal once more. Spring felt along the floor in front of her until she touched the base of the microphone. She stood and spoke - "Good people of Silly Island, please listen to what I am going to ask you to do." Her voice rang loud and clear through the darkness. "Although it's now dark, we are going to start singing and playing again, and we want you to join in. You have heard the words of the song, so please sing them with us. Sing like you have never sung before, loudly, clearly and with as much joy as you can bring to the performance. Sing into the night and we can destroy the darkness. Together we can save Silly Island!"

Although the listeners found it difficult to understand or believe what they were hearing, there was a serious intensity in Spring's voice that stirred them. There were cries of, "Yes!", "Let's do it!", "Come on!", "Hit those notes!" and, as the loudest voice of all from somewhere near the back shouted, "Do it for Silly Island!" Jazz realised it was time for him to play his drums again. Although he couldn't see them, he instinctively knew where each one was positioned, and he played the opening drum roll and cymbal crash before Spring led the singing:

> *"Oh, duck-billed platypus, please stay here with us*
> *Here on Silly Island when it's raining orange juice.*
> *You can stay all day, and then sleep in the hay*
> *Alongside Bertie Buffalo and crazy Monty Moose."*

Wonderfully, everyone joined in. The words started to flow, almost like an electric current, and by the time they reached the chorus there was an amazing mixture of mass singing and laughter:

"Bootle smootle criggety zong,

Angle tangle tiddle, giggle at your sock drawer.

Slippers full of seaweed – yuck!

Chingo bingo wengo tanglesplinge.

Don't forget your knobbly knees,

Fully-grown camels often sneeze.

Barter for a starter, Mister Carter,

Cappy-cap-cap, Gloopy-gloop-gleep.

Never mind the sausages, they don't understand,

Baabaa moomoo neighneigh clang,

Old MacDonald sits on a newspaper.

Wheeeeee, Splat,

BAXTER!"

At the cry of "BAXTER!" the chorus was repeated again, and then again and again until the crazy atmosphere reached a new level of intensity. As the fun continued, the tiny brown-haired creature known as Mister Porridge added to the excitement by sprinting onto the stage, leaping onto one of Jazz's cymbals with a mighty crash, then climbing up the microphone stand before laughing loudly into the microphone for a full ten seconds before dashing off into the night.

Then the most incredible thing of all happened. At the sixth repeat of "BAXTER!" people gradually realised that they could just about see each other again for a few seconds. This unexpected surprise caused a momentary slight reduction in the volume of the singing and laughter, and darkness returned. Spring, realising that her grandfather's ambition might be about to be fulfilled, screamed into the microphone, "Don't stop now - keep going – more, more, more!" The response was immediate, and the previous levels of song and merriment were exceeded as the floodlights flickered once again, and this time the brightness also increased.

Then, as the light became stronger, everyone heard weirdly loud scraping and grating sounds. They were coming from high above the back of the stage. The people all looked into the sky and they could just make out that the 126 metre-long blades of the wind turbine were turning, slowly at first, then gathering pace as the scraping and grating became a whirring, almost purring sound. Handclaps and applause added to the singing and laughter and, for the first time in their lives, the people of Silly Island could actually feel the air move – yes, windy weather was finally being experienced on Silly Island, and the sudden removal and flight of what was left of Hermione's wig was greeted by yet more cheers.

Five minutes later, with the turbine blades now speeding round and round there was an enormous crash as Spring's wonderful painting, unable to cope with all that movement, came clattering to the ground in many pieces. Spring had actually hoped that would happen, because it provided clear proof that Basil's turbine was working.

Needless to say, Spring was juggling again, totally inspired and making up new tricks all the time. Beside her on the stage, Herbie was dancing wildly and his steps, hand actions, turns and expressions were being copied by Lollipop, all the cowsill members, candidates, members of the Herb family and even President Barros.

The celebrations continued for a good hour until Lollipop finally approached the microphone and held up her arms, ready to speak. Jazz, who was by now completely exhausted, dropped his drumsticks and, after a few moments of disappointment that the fun seemed to be over, people realised how tired they all were, and they simply flopped onto the ground.

"Well," began Lollipop, "for the first time in my life I don't know what to say." She paused, then remembered why they had all met there in the first place. "Should we now continue with the election of leader?"

From the left side of the stage, three voices all shouted, "No" and Ed, Hermione and Happyjon came to the microphone.

Happyjon addressed the crowd. "I'm speaking for all three of us: we are withdrawing from the leadership contest. Instead of one of us three becoming your leader, we all want to be in the new cowsill, serving under the incredible Spring Herb, who has saved Silly Island through her brilliant use of science and technology alongside art and music and, of course, silliness. Vote for Spring Herb!"

Ed and Hermione repeated the words, "Vote for Spring Herb!" and the crowd continued to chant Spring's name until Lollipop again approached the microphone.

"Spring Herb is now the only candidate for the leadership of Silly Island, and I declare that she will be your leader for the next five years. Three cheers for Spring Herb and the new cowsill. Hip hip…"

"Hippopotamus," called almost eleven thousand voices.

"Hip hip…"

"Hippopotamus."

"Hip hip..."

"Hippopotamus."

There wasn't a lot of space for the traditional Silly Island dance of celebration, but everyone somehow managed to join in with the necessary six left leg hops followed by seven right leg hops, two claps, four head nods and then star jumps with a massive shout of "Eeksie-peeksie."

Lollipop went on to lead three cheers for Basil Herb, who was overcome by the genuine warmth of all who now knew that his brilliant work could be celebrated at last. He also knew that his wave turbine device could soon be restructured so that the wind and the associated waves could be harnessed to produce yet more electrical energy.

Lollipop also asked for three more cheers, this time for the President of Brazil, although most of the islanders would never know about his humanitarian offer of a new beginning, initially at Rio Silly.

As yet another cry of "Eeksie-peeksie" filled the air, Lollipop made a suggestion that delighted everyone. "Thank you, Silly Islanders, for your enthusiasm and also for supporting me so well for the past five silly years. Before I finally leave my position as leader I have one more idea to put to you. Silly Island has never had a national anthem, but I'm sure you will all agree that the *BAXTER* song would be a great one for us. Do you agree?" The people all roared their approval and started to chant, '*Bax-ter, Bax-ter, Bax-ter, Bax-ter*'.

But some had noticed that the turbine blades were gradually slowing down, and when the floodlights again started to flicker Jazz ran to the front of the stage and spoke into the microphone. "No need to worry, folks." He turned to where Mike and Patty were still happily pedalling and continued, "Spring thought this might happen, and we need never worry about losing power again. Patty, please take the recording back to the beginning of the song and press 'play', then turn up the volume!"

The music, now with the incredible recorded crowd sounds, rang out into the night once more as everyone joined in, the turbine blades spun even faster than before, and the floodlights shone brightly. Lollipop and all those who knew that she had been about to announce devastating news to all the islanders now understood why Spring had spent so much time on her secret project and how she, along with Jazz and Basil, had formulated a plan to provide wind-powered energy after all. Of course, the drumming, juggling and singing had inspired all the laughter, cheering and more singing from the crowd, and Spring's masterful plan to record all those amazing sounds meant that they could be replayed at any time in order to produce energy for Silly Island's needs without coal or any other fossil fuels ever needing to be used again. Silly Island could soon lead the world by using 100% clean energy!

Eventually, after much celebration, the exhausted islanders started to leave Friendly Shirt, happily singing their way to their wind turbine-electrically powered homes. President Barros hugged Lollipop, who told him they must remain friends for life, and he promised to send his famous football team to Silly Island every year.

After she had shaken hands with all those who had been on the stage and were now making their way out of Friendly Shirt, Spring helped Jazz to put away his drum kit and they finally had time to talk to each other. "Well," said Jazz, quietly but excitedly, "you did it."

"No, WE did it," replied Spring. "You were terrific tonight."

"You are going to be a great leader, you know."

"I'll do my best. That's all I can do, after all. But I want to carry on singing and juggling with you too, if that's alright."

"Of course it is!" enthused Jazz, "And I promise to clip the sections of your masterpiece back together for you, not on top of the turbine blades next time, though - I'm sure we'll find the best place to put the painting on display. And I hope you will paint more and more."

"I certainly will! And that reminds me, I need to send a text to someone in Rome, right now, before I turn into a prickly cactus." She paused, then added, "Oh, I don't know why I said that."

Jazz smiled at her, "Maybe it's because you are now the leader of Silly Island!"

Ask the Giraffe

Traditional Silly Island Song

Ask the gi-raffe if you want to know, Ask the gi-raffe be - fore you go,

Ask the gi-raffe if you want to know, How to jump o - ver a fire en - gine.

How to catch a fal-ling snoo-ker ta - ble. How to be an un-der-wa-ter as - tro-naut.

BAXTER!

Silly Island's National Anthem

by Jazz McNoodly-Noodly and Spring Herb

The song is accompanied by drumming only

A drum roll and cymbal clash announce that the song is about to begin

Oh, duck billed plat - y - pus, please stay here with us

Here on Sil - ly Is - land when it's rain - ing o - range juice.

You can stay all day, and then sleep in the hay A

long - side Ber - tie buf - fa - lo and cra - zy Mon - ty Moose.

From this point onwards, half the performers sing the tune

The other half can sing the highest notes possible, screeching as often as they like

They can also make silly sounds and just say the words, or sometimes shout a few of them

Boo - tle smoo - tle crig - ge - ty zong, An - gle tan - gle tid - dle,......

Gig - gle at your sock drawer. Slip - pers full of sea - weed yuck!

Chin - go bin - go wen - go tan - gle - splinge. Don't for - get your

knob - bly   knees,   Ful - ly grown ca - mels   of - ten sneeze.

Bar - ter for a star - ter,____   Mis - ter Car - ter,____   Cap - py - cap - cap,

Gloo - py - gloop - gleep,   Ne - ver mind the sau - sa - ges,   they don't un - der - stand,

Baa - baa moo - moo neigh neigh clang,   Old Mac - Don - ald

sits   on   a   news - pa - per, Wheeee, Splat,   BAX - TER!

Nobody can reach the high notes written for 'BAXTER' but that doesn't matter. Just be silly
Repeat from bar 17 as many times as you like (up to a maximum of 128 times)

Silly Island Quiz

If you have found this page before finishing the book, please stop reading it NOW.

After you have read the whole book, see if you can answer these questions, just for fun!

1 What was Basil Herb's name before he went to live on Silly Island?

A.	Basil Blake
B.	Basil Basic
C.	Frank Plank

2 What was the name of Norman Conquest's 5-wheeled invention?

A.	Bandurple
B.	Gurple
C.	Purple

3 What is the name of Lollipop's husband?

A.	Tom-Tim
B.	Tim-Tom
C.	Tom-Tom

4 What is Mr Acrylic's job?

A.	Miner
B.	Juggling teacher
C.	Art teacher

5 Who is a party organiser?

A.	Jemima Mimer
B.	Hermione Q
C.	Jim Nasium

6 Who organised the Sillylympics?

        A.   Carol Christmas

        B.   Gerald Grainger

        C.   Leighton Early

7 Where is the Sistine Chapel?

        A.   Vatican City

        B.   Friendly Shirt

        C.   Sillytown

8 What is 'The Fly'?

        A.   A fly

        B.   The invisible crow

        C.   An aeroplane

9 Who should you ask if you want to know how to catch a falling snooker table?

        A.   Lollipop McNoodly-Noodly

        B.   The Giraffe

        C.   Mister Porridge

10 Who was referee for the Silly Island v Brazil football match?

        A.   Mick Symonds

        B.   Gerald Grainger

        C.   Hughie Budge

11 Who scored the first goal in the Silly Island v Brazil football match?

        A.   Herbie Herb

        B.   Mike R O'Phone

        C.   It was an own goal, scored by Brazil's number 6

12 Who could you ask for advice if you had a headache?

    A.   Mister Porridge

    B.   Rosemary Herb

    C.   Ed Ache

13 Who is assistant manager at the coal mine?

    A.   Tony Owl

    B.   Tony Crow

    C.   Tony Vulture

14 How does Happyjon Umbrella-Zup perform at Silly Shows?

    A.   He is an upside-down dancer

    B.   He is a wrestler

    C.   He is a drummer

15 Complete this line from the song written by Jazz and Spring: 'Slippers full of seaweed -'

    A.   Splash!

    B.   Lovely!

    C.   Yuck!

16 Who did Rosemary visit for a drink of buttercup coffee?

    A.   February April

    B.   Her friend, Byjingo

    C.   Carol Christmas

17 Where did the Sillylympics take place?

    A.   Sillytown Sillystadium

    B.   Beachy Bay

    C.   Biggety-Big Beach

18 Which instrument does Fredfred MacFred play?
- A. Bagpipes
- B. Drums
- C. Harp

19 Who are the whistling statues?
- A. Phil, Phil, Phil, Bob, Phil and Phil
- B. Phil, Phil, Bob, Phil and Phil
- C. Phil, Phil, Bob, Phil, Phil and Phil

20 Who is Basil Herb's famous friend?
- A. President Barros
- B. Gerald Grainger
- C. Dr Alessandra Cafasso

The answers are upside down on the next page, and they are printed in a different order than the questions, just to make you work a little harder!

Count how many you answered correctly.

This is what your score means:
All 20 correct – Congratulations: you are the world champion!
10 to 20 – Well done - look out of your window NOW and wave to the invisible crow, who is passing by your home at this very moment (you may hear a distant gargling sound)
Less than 10 – A great attempt. Treat yourself to a full afternoon winking at trees
0 – You didn't really read the book at all, did you?
More than 20 – You are very silly indeed!

Answers:

16 B) Her friend, Byjingo 20 C) Dr Alessandra Cafasso 2 B) Gurple 7 A) Vatican City 10 A) Mick Symonds 18 A) Bagpipes 11 C) It was an own goal, scored by Brazil's number 6 5 A) Jemima Mimer 8 C) An aeroplane 13 A) Tony Owl 17 B) Beachy Bay 4 C) Art teacher 1 A) Basil Blake 12 C) Ed Ache 15 C) Yuck! 6 C) Leighton Early 9 B) The Giraffe 19 C) Phil, Phil, Bob, Phil, Phil and Phil 14 A) He is an upside-down dancer 3 B) Tim-Tom

About the Author

Former teacher and headteacher, Brian Beresford, is an author and children's songwriter. Brian has visited many schools, reading excerpts from his first children's book, 'The Midnight Grocer', which has proved to be a favourite of many. He hopes that his new comedy, 'Silly Island', will bring joy to all its readers.

Cover illustrations and design by BazMac

Acknowledgement

Brian wishes to thank his publisher, Lionel Ross, for his support, encouragement and enthusiasm, and also to Roy Clayton for his expertise as editor.